Season's Meetings

DEVIN AUDRAH

Season's Meetings

DEVIN AUDRAH

The WindWord Group Publishing & Media
#324, 1083 N. Collier Boulevard
Marco Island, Florida, 34145
USA

http://www.windwordgroup.com

ISBN: 978-1-947527-18-8

SEASON'S MEETINGS

In memory of
the late Maeve Binchy

DEVIN AUDRAH

CHAPTER 1

Fifth Avenue was as magical as any Christmas movie would have you believe. Snow decorated the sidewalks with a sparkling carpet and holiday glit-ter adorned many of the storefront windows.

If only Noelle could keep her footing! These slippery-sole shoes were all wrong for Manhattan sidewalks in December.

Yesterday at home in Vermont, she had decided that the heavy treads on her hiking boots would look too unstylish and that these lighter shoes were a good combination of comfort and looks. A week ago, when the sidewalks were bare, they would have been fine for NYC. But today, these shoes had her skidding around like a sled on an icy hill. Her only other choices were a pair of flats or the pair of heels she'd brought to go with her dress on Christmas Day. It was going to be a long week.

Their progress was slow, but they were still making better time than they would have in a taxi.

"Nonny! Stop grabbing my coat!" Kelsey came to a full stop in front of a pizza place, her pale little face set in a determined frown and her eyes the color of an ocean just before a storm.

Kelsey was only four years old, but she knew how to stake out her turf. She wanted to stop at every doorway and look it over.

"Stay close to me, Kenneth," Noelle said to the little girl's older brother. "Let's let Kelsey be the leader for a while."

Long after she had had her fill of elves, reindeer, and Santa figurines, her grandchildren were still entranced by the window displays. Noelle's mind was on auto-pilot, and she almost missed the Nutcracker Ballet poster, dozens of copies of it plastered up on a construc-tion hoarding. "Oh, kids, this would be fun!"

"What is it?" Kenneth was suspicious, staring at the photograph of a gloriously glittery Sugar Plum Fairy.
"It's a very famous ballet that dancers in cities all over the world perform every year. It has fairies, and a prince, and a battle, and beautiful music."

"Dancing?" He was only six, but Kenneth knew how to roll his eyes.

This was going sideways. "It's like Princess Anna and Princess Elsa have a play date with a soldier. On Christmas Eve. A toy comes to life, and there's a magician. And a giant Christmas tree!"

Kelsey came to a full stop and the river of walkers that filled the entire sidewalk parted to go around this tiny obstacle. "A tree! We have to get our tree."
Somehow, Noelle doubted that decorating a tree was in her

daughter and son-in-law's plan for the week. Georgia and Kyle seemed to be buried in work.

"Well, there are Christmas trees everywhere, aren't there? There is a really big one, back in the hotel lobby, and there's a huge one at Rockefeller Center that I'll take you to see tomorrow."

"Today! Today!" The little ones chanted.
"But today, Santa is waiting for us over at the department store!" Noelle said. "At the North Pole, at his workshop!"

That settled it. Now, they were a team of three, all rowing toward the store.

**

Noelle guided the two kiddies onto the department store escalator, and as they rose to the second floor, past eight-foot-long hanging cardboard snow-flakes, she felt her own excitement growing. The toy department on the Saturday afternoon before Christmas was a hive of very industrious bees, all crawling in and out of tiny, crowded spaces, trying to gather the necessary supplies and bring them home to the queen.

Maybe it was the wrong place to take the grandkids, but Kyle and Georgia had left it up to her and this was what would thrill Kenneth and Kelsey. Besides, Noelle still needed to find those mini-GPT3 robot things that the little ones wanted from Santa.

She stared at the wonderland of lights decorating the North Pole and engulfing trees of a dozen different sizes. Brightly wrapped packages sur-rounded the trees and cascaded from the shelves.

And so much movement! Toy trains raced around tracks, spacecraft and drones whizzed by overhead, and knee-high robots cruised among the shoppers.

At the end of a magnificent boulevard set up between the superheroes and the board games, Santa's throne awaited the jolly gentleman's butt. A huge red sack filled with packages lay beside the chair, ready to stoke the imagination of the child who hadn't yet grasped the concept.

The latest toys were on display on pedestals, ready to give ideas to any children who were still adding to their wish lists.

Children in a frenzy of anticipation cruised the aisles while their parents tried to keep track of the things that caught their attention.

Noelle's attention was seized by a tall man who seemed to stand off to one side, assessing the scene. It wasn't any one thing about him; it was the way he carried himself, with an air of confidence and command.

Maybe he was the store detective, watching out for shoplifters? Or maybe some famous actor she should recognize, out at a store, incognito. Maybe he was watching the Santa Claus action, picking up details for his next role?

She was getting silly, and letting her mind wander in a way she really shouldn't, while she had the kiddies with her. Kelsey spotted a display of garish Christmas sweaters, sized from toddlers to Triple X. "Look, Nonny! Let's get those!" She tugged at Noelle's hand.

Kenneth was already in fourth gear, heading for the toy cars display. "Hold on there, Speedy," Noelle said. "Let's just stop here for a minute."

Noelle let Kelsey make a choice, then picked up a matching one for her-self. Kenneth nodded when she showed him one with a tough-looking reindeer landing on a snowy mountaintop, and she guided them over to the cash register.

Her credit cards were starting to groan under the weight of her Christmas spending so far but she still had miles to go: ballet tickets, tips for the hotel staff, dinner out to thank Georgia and Kyle for hosting her. And one more gift for each of the grandkids: the elusive mini-GPT3.

The outsized dollar sign on the notice beside the cash register caught her attention. "Last day to enter! Guess Santa's middle name and win $5000. And a mini-GPT3! (IF we can find one)."

"Now, wouldn't that help with balancing the checkbook at this time of year." A tall man in a classic camelhair top coat who was in front of her in the line turned to smile into her eyes. He was looking at her as if he knew her.

It made Noelle uncomfortable—she couldn't say whether it was in a good way. Besides, what business was it of his, how much or how little she had to spend?

He looked vaguely familiar, too. Oh, wait a minute! She had it! He was the boss-type man she'd noticed earlier, the one who looked like he might be picking up research, as an actor. Or casing the joint, for a robbery?

Really, her imagination was out of control.

She ignored him, but he persisted. "Santa's middle name, huh? I'm very sure he doesn't have one, but it's a clever concept. My guess is there's no 'right' answer. They'll just give the prize to whoever comes up with something really entertaining."

Noelle tightened her cheeks in a blank half-smile and let the strains of "Jingle Bells" on the store's festive playlist drift through her mind. She wanted to try to stay in the Christmas mood. Plus, she didn't want this man to know that she was yearning for an extra few thousand dollars.

Noelle finished her ugly sweaters transaction and turned her back as decisively as she could.

But he wasn't giving up or going away. "Ma'am? Do you mind—"

Ma'am! Cremees in a cone, she hated being called that. Especially by a guy who was at least as old as she was. Maybe even ten years older.

"Ma'am, they're motioning for you to move aside. I think they're trying to keep this area clear."

What was he talking about?

Kenneth pulled at her hand, also demanding her attention. "Nonny! Santa's coming!"

"Your grandson has it right, ma'am. This is the direction Santa Claus comes from when he's ready to sit over there on his throne and meet with all the children who've lined up to see him." He spoke as if he knew what he was talking about. "Or perhaps not your grandson? Your son?"

She turned to give him a good look. Well. Drop-dead gorgeous. A silver fox, as Sherry would say. Broad shoulders, eyes that almost matched his dark-blue tie, hands of a piano player.

"And why would you happen to know about Santa's route through the toy department?"

"Special security, ma'am."

A-ha. Now she got it.

"Do you think you could stop calling me 'ma'am'?"

He grinned boyishly and she had a nano-second of believing that he was calling her that just to get a rise out of her. As it happened, it worked. She grinned back: ten points for you, buddy. Game on.

Noelle tucked herself and the two kiddies in between the glass counter and six-foot-tall Christmas tree, just off the candy-cane-red carpet that led to the Santa's Workshop command chair.

"You know what I think?" He'd followed them over to their spot.

"About what?" she asked.

"Santa's middle name."

Noelle hadn't meant to get into a conversation with this man, but . . . here she was. "All right, Mr. Santa Expert. What do you think?"

"I think it's Clarence."

"Well, maybe George Bailey," Noelle said, before she realized he was kneeling down to talk to her grandson.

Kenneth grinned. "Clarence. I like that."

"Maybe Michael," Noelle said. If it was angel-movies, she could keep up.

The man kept his head down near Kenneth's. "Maybe it's Hee-haws."

This put the little guy into giggles. "Santa Hee-haws Claus, that's good."

"Or Paws."

Kelsey was not about to be left out. "Santa Paws Claus!"

The man had a couple of the entry forms in his hand.

Matt Kezanski.

A growing buzz to their right drew everyone's gaze down the red carpet toward what Noelle guessed was the storage area. Two swinging doors burst open, the volume of the Christmas carols on the overhead speakers cranked way up, and a large, pot-bellied, white-whiskered man in a high-quality Santa suit walked slowly through the crowd of kids and parents, shaking hands, patting heads, and beaming at his fans.

It only took about twenty seconds for him to reach his chair, but Noelle estimated he talked to thirty kids before he got there. A lineup of forty more waited in line to sit on his knee and make their pitch for a new doll or video game.

Or a mini-GPT3. Maybe Santa was the one who had cornered the market?

She looked down at Kelsey, whose little face was glowing.

"So, what's your best guess for his middle name?"

His voice was above her right ear, rather than down near her knee this time. "I'd like it to be Santa 'Bringer of mini-GPT3 toys' Claus."

"Ah. Are you looking everywhere for one of those, too?"

"Three of them. One for my other grandson, Frost. One for this one. And Kelsey wants one, too." Noelle looked down at the little girl beside her.

Who was this?

"Kenneth, where's Kelsey?" Her head swung back and forth as she looked over every one of the little girls standing nearby. Kenneth either didn't hear her or was so mesmerized by the sight of Santa that her words didn't register.

It was time to shout.

"Kelsey!" She looked around for something to step up on, some way to make herself taller and get her head up higher than the crowd. This couldn't be happening! Noelle called three more times, her voice rising even louder than the excited buzz around Santa's arrival.

A woman standing in the center of a group of four other little girls picked up on the vibe.

"What's wrong? What is it?"
"My granddaughter is missing!"

Noelle looked frantically around the crowd, searching for Kelsey's red hair and blue coat.

She felt like throwing up.

CHAPTER 2

The man pulled his phone from his pock-et. "She can't have gone far," he said to Noelle, then began tapping the screen to send a text.

Noelle gripped Kenneth's hand, then rocked from foot to foot, trying to decide what to do next. Should she hunt for her, go up and down the aisles? The place was so packed with people. . . how would she ever spot her? Should she scream her name, over and over?

"They've got the doors closed and the department sealed off," the man told her. What was his name, again? "They'll need a full description. Do you have a photo?"

Noelle let go of Kenneth, then groped through her purse. She didn't take her eyes off the little boy for a second. He took the photo. "And her name is Kelsey? And you are . . . "

"Noelle Moran."

"Don't worry, Noelle. We'll find her."

Kenneth had a plan. "I'm going to go look for her."

"No!" Noelle grabbed for his hand. "You stay right here by me."

The man squatted beside the little boy. "Your grandma needs you to help her here, son," he said. "I'll find your sister." He straightened up. "Give me your number. I'll text you when we find her." And he was gone.

Matt, that was it. Matt Kezanski.

Noelle felt hysteria rise in her throat. The room was spinning and the people around her were going out of focus.

She felt someone walk her a few feet to a chair. Kenneth was almost glued to her side and after she sank down to sit, he leaned against her and put a little arm around her waist. A store clerk appeared with a glass of wa-ter for Noelle.

A buzz spread through the crowd, and even though Santa continued to re-ceive his little visitors, parents in the lineup gripped their kids tightly. Noelle clutched her phone, glancing down at the screen every few minutes, looking for Matt's text.

She didn't know how long she sat there, she and Kenneth holding onto each other. It felt like forever.

"Excuse me, could I speak to you for a moment? You're Ms. Moran, the little girl's grandmother?"

She turned to see a big, black camera lens pointing at her. The man beside it was holding a TV news microphone.

They recognized each other in-stantly.

"You remember me from the air-port? Wow, small world."

She certainly did remember him from the airport when she'd arrived on the plane from Vermont. Not every day you see somebody in real life that you see on your TV screen almost every night.

"I'm Dan Keyes from Channel 45 News. I was at the Empire State Build-ing, working on a feature, when my editor sent me over here. The police have an alert out and we thought it might help if we could get the word out to everyone to be on the lookout for her."

Dear God. Was that necessary? Kelsey was nearby. She must be. It would only be minutes until she was back here and everything was okay. It had to be. Noelle took a closer look at this newsman. His smile looked friendly, but she couldn't quite catch his eyes, as he was scanning the crowd, muttering into his cell phone, and speaking to her, all at the same time.

"I just did a call-in to interrupt regular programming. We're going to have everyone in the city watching for her."

They waited as the minutes ticked by.

"Nonny! Nonny!"

And there she was! Noelle turned toward Kelsey's voice and saw her com-ing down one of the toy aisles, holding onto Matt's hand. She let go to run into her grandmother's arms. The crowd in the Santa lineup burst into applause.

"Where were you, honey?" Noelle asked.

"With Santa!"

"They found her behind the chair, tucked in under the fabric flap, so no one could see her." Matt's eyes were shining, his smile broad and happy.

The faces all around them looked equally delighted. She felt unfamiliar hands pat her on the shoulder and heard an excited hum as the families got back to the business of seeing Santa and planning their gift-giving.

"Mom!" Georgia rushed toward Noelle, followed by Kyle and his mother Pamela. Every one of the strands of Pamela's ash-blonde hair was holding its place in perfect style and she looked as though she could be on the cover of a magazine. The flawless grandmother. Why was Noelle noticing something like that at a time like this?

Georgia was disheveled and upset. "Where is she? Is she all right? Are you alright? Oh, here you are, baby. Someone in the meeting saw the news alert and we came right over." Georgia dropped to her knees and threw her arms around Kelsey.

"I think she's going to be right as rain," Matt said. "Maybe a little over-whelmed with all this attention."

Georgia stood up. "Are you the one who found her?"

Dan stepped forward. "That was my news alert you saw," he said. "Do you think we could do a brief interview? Let everyone know we found her?"

Kelsey looked up at him from her spot up against Georgia's leg. "I found myself. I had to go to the bathroom, and I didn't think Santa could take me. So, I came out."

"How did she wander off?" Pamela reached out to pat Kelsey on the head, as if she were a pet dog. Not a particularly beloved dog, either.

"I wouldn't say she wandered. I was paying for some sweaters and she was beside me at the sales desk. I took my eyes off her for a second and she was gone."

Dan turned to the camera lens and signaled for his cameraman to start roll-ing while he did his report. "A happy ending in the Toy Department this afternoon" was his closing remark. Then, Noelle watched the camera pan toward Santa, who tossed in a hearty "ho ho ho."

She felt exhausted and she could see that Georgia looked drained, too.

But the kiddies seemed not at all wiped out by the experience. After Santa said hello to each of them and heard their direct pitch for a mini GPT3 robot, they let themselves be herded toward the escalator. Noelle looked back to thank Matt Kezanski, but she couldn't see him anywhere in the crowd.

Kyle flagged down two cabs outside the store and by the time they arrived back at the hotel, Noelle was ready for a break.

"I think a long hot bath would be a good idea," she said, as they walked back into the suite. Was it really only seven hours since she'd walked out her front door in Burlington this morning?

"Oh, that's a perfect idea, Mom, thank you. The kids' PJs are in their room. Could you put them in those right after they're finished their bath? Kelsey needs her rubber duckie and Kenneth has two boats. I'll order some supper from Room Service. I still have a few things to finish up from the meeting this afternoon."

Pamela strolled over to the side-board near the table in the dining area. Half a dozen crystal decanters, filled with various shades of amber liquid, covered its marble top.

She helped herself to a glass of something and waved it in Georgia's direction. "Don't you worry about entertaining me. I'll be fine out here with a magazine while you and Kyle finish up your work."

Noelle forced herself to count to ten slowly and keep

her thoughts to herself.

She knew she'd have to forgive Georgia for her presumption, too. After all, there had been a thousand bath times that she'd never been able to share with Kenneth and Kelsey. Shouldn't she be thrilled that she could take over with this one?

The three of them had a blast, floating toy ships, sinking rubber duckies, and making mermaids dive into the bath-water. They'd worked up quite an appetite by the time they came out of the bedroom, kids with their flannel pajamas and Noelle with her blouse and pants damp from all the splashing.

There was no sign of any supper. Pamela's coat had disappeared from the couch where she'd thrown it and her boots were gone from the mat by the door.

Noelle could hear Kyle and Georgia's voices in the office area of the suite; it sounded as though they were on the phone again.

She turned to the children and gave them her best smile. "Hey, you two! Who wants cookies?"

"Well, we're the only two here, so I guess it's us," Kenneth said with the earnest logic of a six-year-old.

Noelle grinned. "Then I guess you're the two who get to try these world-famous thumbprint cookies. Come on, let's go to my room and get them out of my suitcase."

"What are thumbprint cookies?"

Noelle pulled her bag out from under the cot. "It's a cookie that you make by pressing your thumb down into the dough before you bake it," she said. "I got them from my friend by trading for some of my Nanaimo bars."

"Are we having Nanaimo bars, too?" Kelsey asked.

"Oh, yes, I brought some of those along, too. I have enough cookies for us to try a different kind every day while we're here, waiting for Christmas Day," Noelle said.

"Mmm, they're good, these thumbing cookies," Kelsey mumbled through her mouthful.

Kenneth took a handful of four and headed back to the living room. He picked up the TV remote control and found himself an action-hero cartoon. It was amazing how comfortable these little kids were with technology.

Noelle and Kelsey followed along and joined him on the couch. Kelsey seemed none the worse for her adventure in the store.

Kenneth seemed a little put out by all the attention his sister was getting, but he'd get over it. It seemed that her disappearance had been just a minor blip on the radar of the family's day. Noelle thought that of the five of them, she was the one most shaken up by the experience.

Georgia appeared and carried the two little ones off to bed. Kyle changed the channel to see the news.

"Today in Manhattan, the parent's nightmare came true when a four-year-old went missing from the lineup to see Santa Claus," the newscaster said. "Dan Keyes has the story."

Noelle froze, then took a close look. There, on the bottom of the screen, was that TV reporter's name, Dan Keyes, and across the top Saturday, 2:45 p.m.

During a slow pan of the crowd and the toy department, Dan's voice told the story of Kelsey's adventure. Nice voice. The report ended with a close-up of Santa smiling for the camera.

Noelle looked over at Kyle. He was scrolling through his phone messages and paying no attention. The sound of laughter came from Kenneth and Kelsey's bedroom, where Georgia was reading them a story.

A few hours later, after Noelle helped tuck the little ones into bed, she pulled out her phone to call Yvonne. "You know, maybe this is good for me, to spend time with these younger, very flexible people," she said. "There's just no time to brood about how upset I was or how horrible it would have been if it had turned into a disaster."

"Maybe." Yvonne didn't sound convinced. For many years now, she had been dubious about Georgia and Kyle's work schedules.

"Anyway, all's well that ends well, and everybody is back here, safe and sound."

"What's tomorrow?" Yvonne asked. "Are you all going to see the sights of New York?"

"Georgia and Kyle might have to work and they've asked me to be on standby to look after the kids."

"Really. Work," Yvonne said. "On Sunday."

"Yvonne. You're not going to criticize them for their lack of religious respect?"

"No, I'm not going to criticize them at all, Noelle. She's your daughter and it's your Sunday afternoon. I shouldn't have said anything." There were spaces the size of skyscrapers between the lines of what she was saying.

In the city less than twenty-four hours, and already Noelle was regretting her decision to go there.

CHAPTER 3

48 Hours Earlier

Noelle had never had much use for her first name. She didn't know why her parents had given it to her and she'd never asked. Now that her mother was gone, too, there wouldn't be an opportunity.

It wasn't because of her birthday—her birthday was in July. Maybe her mother had wanted a Christmas baby. Maybe she was just bent on choosing something unusual. Everyone, from teachers in school to order-takers on the phone, grabbed the chance to make a joke.

"The First? Yes, The First Noël," she'd say, with as much of a smile as she could manage on that particular day.

It happened a lot more at this time of the year. As soon as Thanksgiving was history and the Christmas carols appeared on the radio and in the air at the mall, Noelle could expect a snicker almost every time she gave someone her name.

'Twas the season to be jolly, though, and it was Christmas party time. She pulled into Yvonne's driveway, the windshield wipers going at full speed against the falling snow.

It was only five o'clock, but darkness had invaded this quiet Burlington street. Yvonne's house lit it up, though, the front door decorated in red and green garland, and strings of multi-colored lights outlining all of the windows. Yvonne was what Noelle would call a moderate Christmas fan: not over-the-top, like Isabel, and not semi-Grinch, the name Noelle was occasionally called when the three friends got together.

Yvonne was ready to go, on time as always. The door opened and she stepped out in a red parka. Were those green boots? A little strange, not a good look for most women of a certain age, but somehow, it worked when Yvonne did it. She carried her usual massive shoulder bag and a cookie tin.

Noelle left the headlights on as a guide through the late afternoon dusk. Yvonne took her time, navigating the icy steps, holding the railing with one hand. She pulled open the passenger door and ushered in a blast of frigid air.

"Hi, Yvonne. Ready to rock 'n' roll?" Noelle was worried that it would be a challenge getting home later. "What do you think, should we be going out in this weather? Isabel's place is kind of off the main drag."

"That's an understatement. But yes, of course, we should." Yvonne settled into the minivan's front seat and snapped in her seatbelt. "She's expecting us and you know she has every one of her eight dozen Christmas decorations out, her ugly sweater on, and the carols going full blast."

Noelle laughed. "On the turntable, no doubt. She told me the other day, that she's back into vinyl."

"I would think that would be something you'd like."

"Well, you're right, Yvonne, I do. There's a lot of things from the '60s and '70s that were excellent, and one of them was music on vinyl. It just sounds better, don't you think? That's why even the kids today are discovering it."

"I agree with you, but you can't argue with the convenience of the mp3s and the music subscription services."

Noelle sighed. "There's been a lot to keep up with. A lot of change. I have days when I think that I just don't want to learn anything anymore. Not another device, not another app, not one more thing!"

"Oh, don't turn into an old grump, Noelle, for heaven's sake!" This was a frequent theme of Yvonne's. It was more than slightly amusing because she was the oldest.

"What are you talking about? I'm not an old grump. I am totally adaptable to change."

"Yeah, right." Yvonne snuggled down into her warm coat. Vermont winters were no joke.

"Wow, this snow is really coming down."

"Just take it easy and we'll get there. Like I told Sam when I left, a party is a party. You can't just not show up." Yvonne watched over the seat as Noelle backed down the driveway. "Whoa. How many cookie tins do you have back there? You do get the concept, don't you? You bring a dozen cookies from your best recipe, the secret one you've been refusing to share since the '70s, and you get to swap for someone else's best."

"Unless you're Sherry and you only have time to stop by the supermarket and pick up a bag of chewy chocolate chip."

"Which you then trade for something incredibly exotic that cost somebody three dollars a cookie to make!"

Noelle managed to control her instinct to take her eyes off the road and look at Yvonne while they both laughed. The snow was coming down like confetti and she could barely see a thing. "I get the concept, Yvonne. But I brought a few extra because I want to trade for a big collection. I'm taking them to my grandchildren tomorrow for Christmas and I want there to be seven, one for each day I'm there."

"You're over-achieving, Noelle! Seven tins of cookies, my God! Are you taking four suitcases? Look, it doesn't have to be a performance and you don't have to win the Olympics of cookies. They're little kids, they'll enjoy you no matter what you bring."

"You don't have grandkids."

"Are you suggesting that means I don't get an opinion?" Yvonne laughed. "Because I do."

Isabel's house was at the end of a long driveway lined by tightly planted pine trees that were a delight in the August sunshine and protection in a December storm.

She had created a Christmas extravaganza, with lights twinkling on every branch of every tree, replica reindeer positioned every few yards, and a sleigh by the front door, adorned with red lights as the grand finale. Half a dozen parked cars signaled that Isabel's annual Christmas cookie swap party was well-attended, despite the storm.

An hour later, Noelle had surveyed all the others' contributions and had traded tins of her specialty, peppermint Nanaimo bars, for tins of thumbprints, shortbread, sugar, volcano, and sandwich cookies, krispie mashups, and gingerbread reindeer, unicorns, and dinosaurs. Amazing. There were cookie cutter shapes for everything these days.

She caught sight of a tray of date squares and dithered over her choices: maybe the sugar cookies should go back?

"The grandkids will like the sugar cookies with all that icing more than the other ones." Sherry's words telegraphed so much self-confidence, the same way her red dress and high heels did.

"How did you know I'm thinking about my grandkids?" Noelle asked.

"Because you always are," Sherry said. She had her head bent over a small notepad on the table beside the sugar cookie tray. "Did you vote yet?"

"Vote on what?"

"Isabel wants us to vote for the best cookie. Try a sample, then write your favorites, first, second, and third. Ha! I see that gleam in your eye, Noelle Moran."

"Well, my peppermint Nanaimo bars are pretty special."

"I think I'm going to vote for anything with green sparkles that match my boots," Yvonne said, as she walked up with an open box and tongs in her hands. "What do we have here, ladies? Sugar cookies, fully iced? Five hundred calories each?"

"Oh, at least," Sherry laughed. "Probably more like a thousand."

Noelle bit into a sugar cookie shaped like an elf, with a garish red-and-white striped hat and matching shoes. She got a kick out of biting off its head. Sometimes, it was a bit too much, all this Christmas glitz, and it got to her.

Demolishing an elf felt good, somehow. "This one tastes pretty good."

"Come on now, you know you want to win," Yvonne said.

"Well, if that's what Noelle wants, that's what Noelle gets," Sherry said. "I'm going to go stuff the ballot box. But, listen, before I do, I just want to talk to you about something. You remember I mentioned my friend at work? Ronny? The one who got divorced a couple years back?"

Noelle was leery. "Yeah . . . "

"He told me yesterday that he needs a date for his daughter's wedding in a couple of months and I thought of you."

"No, Sherry."

"Come on, Noelle, give it a little thought. It's perfect, really. You can go out with him a time or two, see if there's any chemistry, and still leave him with tons of time to find somebody else, if there's not." Sherry nibbled at a piece of shortbread. "I had no idea he was still single. I thought for sure somebody would have snapped him up by now. He has a nice house on the south side; we were all there for the company Fourth of July party. Big yard, cute dog. He cooks—well, barbecues, anyway."

"No, Sherry."

"Noelle, come on. He's healthy, the ex-wife is not a lunatic, his adult children live on the west coast and there aren't any grandchildren, that I know of. Or sisters or mother still living."

"Can you give us a rundown on his bank account? How about his medical history?" Yvonne asked.

"Well, he did have——" Sherry stopped when she saw the two of them laughing. "You're messing with me. All right, Noelle, but I'm telling you, he's a nice guy and you could do a lot worse."

"I don't think I want to 'do' at all."

"Why ever not?" Sherry asked.

Noelle just shook her head.

"Well, I do have to go vote for cookies. But you let me know if you change your mind, you hear?" Sherry set off toward the kitchen.

Yvonne watched her go. "Did you tell me you two had a tiff last week?"

Noelle took the tongs from Yvonne and concentrated on picking up the cookies one by one, gently placing them in a tin. "Yeah, we did. We're going on a road trip in the spring and she wants to plan the whole thing. I suggested a slightly different itinerary and she got really huffy."

"Why do you put up with that?"

"Well, she's Sherry, right?" Since high school, she'd been 'that's-Sherry-that's-how-she-is'.

Noelle believed in accepting a friend for her good qualities and letting the small stuff go, but Yvonne saw it differently.

"You let her boss you around too much."

"Well, we're close. I don't have anyone, you know. Since Ian passed. You have Sam and Izzie has Rob." Noelle looked across the room. "Aha! No lineup for the gingerbread right now. Gotta go. I'm on a mission."

The aroma of fresh-baked ginger-bread was almost intoxicating. Noelle was right in the middle of a deep breath when her phone buzzed and the contact display showed Georgia's photo.

Noelle often felt as if she were looking in a mirror when she saw her daughter's photo, except for the red hair that came from Ian's side of the family. The brown eyes and big smile came from Noelle's side.

"Hey Georgia."

"Hey Mom. What're you doing?"

"I'm at a Christmas cookie swap party at Isabel's. Picking up a few things to bring with me tomorrow to your place."

"That's why I'm calling, Mom. There's been a change of plan."

Noelle felt her energy level crash. Maybe it was just a sugar drop, after all the sampling she'd been doing? No, it was in response to Georgia. Definitely. "What change of plan?"

"I know you were going to drive down to our place, but it turns out that Kyle and I have to be in New York for some business meetings."

"Business meetings during Christmas week?" Noelle rolled her eyes at Yvonne, then backed away from all the activity in the kitchen and dining room to a quiet chair in the living room.

"It's the company Christmas party, actually. We were going to give it a pass but some things have come up and it's starting to look like we really need to be there."

"But the kids—"

"Oh, we're taking the kids, too. Of course. Mom, we know it's awfully last-minute for you to make other plans."

Noelle had a fleeting thought of herself sitting with

Yvonne and Sam beside their tree on Christmas morning. Even worse, she might be in a room full of Isabel and Rob's extended family—kids, grandkids, aunts, uncles, and cousins.   Thank goodness, Sherry had booked a cruise to St. Thomas and wouldn't be one of the ones pity-pressuring Noelle to join her.

Maybe that's what she should do. Take a cruise or some other holiday. As soon as that idea hit her mind, Noelle felt like her heart was encased in a con-crete block. She needed to be with old friends or family at Christmas.

But it was a bit too late to ask Daisy if she would be welcome. Daisy wouldn't like being second choice after her sis-ter.

"I know you've been busy, Mom, with your Christmas activities, your book club and yoga and things—"

"Georgia, we just talked last night about the holiday plans! And the very next day, you're telling me you're changing them?"

"I didn't plan it this way, Mom. But things do come up, and we have to be flexible."

"But, Georgia . . . Christmas!"

"Mom, we want you to come with us."

Wait, what?

"To New York?"

"Yes, New York."

"New York City at Christmas."

"Yes, did you ever do that? When Dad was still alive?"

"No, never. Dad didn't like to travel, and I've never been a big fan of New York."

"Or of too much Christmas fuss. I remember. But

come on, Mom, it could be fun."

"I did a lot of preparation for coming to your place," Noelle said. "I was going to hit the road for Cincinnati first thing in the morning. I have gifts, and tins of cookies, and—"

"So, you can bring cookies to New York. They won't mind! And you can ship the gifts, or bring them with you on the plane."

"On the plane?"

"Yes, we're going to send you a ticket. And we have a room for you at the hotel. Wait till you see it. Our new company chose it and it's gorgeous."

"I'll have to think about it, Geor-gia."

"Don't think too long, Mom. Come on, it will be so much fun. I know it's short notice but being flexible keeps you young, right? . . . Oh, just a second, Kelsey needs help with her shoe-laces. Mom, I have to go. Call me by tomorrow, okay?"

Noelle couldn't keep her mind on anything else for the rest of the evening. She barely noticed Isabel's raised eyebrows or Yvonne's shake of her head when she told them about her holiday change of plans.

She couldn't even bring herself to celebrate winning second place in the cookie contest and she didn't feel her usual fire over losing at something.

On the drive home, Yvonne tried to get her to laugh by suggesting they eat most of the cookies to make themselves feel better. The snow had stopped falling by the time she pulled back into her own driveway at eight. She'd planned to heat some leftover pasta for a late dinner, but after the taste of the cookies and the disappointment, she had no appetite.

Noelle sat down in front of her gas fire-place, flipped it on, and stared into the fake flame. A glass of red wine, that's what she needed. A glass of wine and a few tears.

She let herself give in.

Only half an hour after purging the bad stuff, her head was packed again with the worries. The worries that her grandkids wouldn't know her because she lived too far away. That her friends were only spending time with her out of pity. That their time for her had a limit, and it was approaching. That she'd be left all alone, to be discovered days after she was dead from something easily cured.

Noelle picked up her glass and began a tour of the house. She stopped in the kitchen to put the seven cookie tins in the freezer, then pulled open the pantry door to look at the rows of boxes of pasta, rice, and walnuts. Very uninspiring.

The next stop was the mirror in the front hall. Boring, just like her food supplies. Gray hair, cut sensibly short, a dusting of freckles over her nose and cheeks, a few wrinkles but not too many—not a dried-apple look, but enough to remind everybody that she was a fall chicken, maybe even a winter one.

Where did that phrase 'no spring chicken' come from, anyway?

She stared into her own eyes. This was not a face to stop a clock or launch a thousand ships. Where were all these old sayings coming from? They came to mind more readily than what she'd had for breakfast or where she'd put her favorite watch.

Noelle laughed at herself and took another healthy swig of the wine. The trouble was that when she looked in the mirror, she didn't really recognize the woman looking back. Inside, she felt like her eighteen-year-old self. In the mirror, she was locking eyes with a stranger.

But she wasn't eighteen, she was fifty-five. She looked it and she knew how to act it. Ever since Ian died ten years ago, she'd made a quiet life for herself and she had no expectations of any-thing different. If she occasionally carped about the lack of excitement or love in her life, well, she was just over-reacting to some movie, TV show, or book that was stirring her up unneces-sarily.

She had her health, her friends, and her family; she should be grateful. Love and excitement were for the young.

Focus on what you have, not on what you don't have. And what she had was an invitation to New York to spend Christmas with her grandchildren!

When the morning broke, she got on the phone. "I've made up my mind, dear. I'll take you up on your invitation."

"Mom, that's awesome! We'll meet you at JFK tomorrow afternoon."

"How will you get there so fast?"

"We're here already, flew in from Cincinnati last night," Georgia said. "I'll email your ticket as soon as I get off the phone."

Noelle went to the storage closet and pulled out her smaller suitcase. After pondering, she switched it for the biggest one, the one that would have room for all the cookies.

**

The traffic at the airport in New York was thick, both inside and out. Noelle set her jaw and put her head down. The only way to get through this scene was with determination.

Why did the movies about New York show it as this magical, energetic place, filled with terrific buildings, parks, and people? The movies were made by people who loved the city, obviously.

Noelle wasn't one of those. She had only visited once before, when her turn had come up to shepherd a group of thirty middle school kids on a field trip. They were going to see art at the Metropolitan Museum.

Most of the school trips were within a few hundred miles of Burlington. Somehow, Noelle had been one of the teachers who drew a straw for the New York trip, and even though it had only been a weekend, it was down in her memory as one of the most exhausting, unpleasant experiences of her life.

Of course, a lot of the memories had to do with the challenges of wrangling thirty twelve-year-old kids in and out of buses, hotels, and subway cars, but a lot of it also had to do with New York itself. She hadn't liked it then, and she didn't like it now.

Within ten minutes of touching down, she was missing home. The rolling hills, the lake, the trees, the low-key vibe downtown—it was home, and Noelle had never yearned for anything dif-ferent. Oh, yes, well, of course, there were times when she had a bit of cabin fever. Everybody did, anywhere you were. She didn't pay much attention to that, just let it pass.

She shuffled along with the crowd, eve-ryone packed in shoulder to shoulder, like salmon swimming upstream to spawn.

At the baggage carousel, Noelle hung back until she saw her plaid suit-case roll by. How did those cookies handle the trip? She edged closer, trying to find a spot to claim in the midst of the hundreds of people reaching for their bags.

After a year of missing out on holiday travel to be with family and friends, Americans had returned to their pre-COVID-19 airport enthusiasm by the millions. It felt like every one of them was right here in Noelle's personal space.

She lunged forward, reaching for her bag and was surprised to see a long, masculine arm in a fleece jacket reach past her and grasp its handle. Well, my, my. Whether he was helping because he liked her, because he wanted to help all female passersby, or more likely, because she reminded him of his mother, Noelle appreciated his move.

At least, that's how she felt until he pulled the suit-case to his side, checked the tag, and realized it wasn't his. He straightened up and walked back to the baggage carousel.

Noelle reached down to take control of her bag. Oh well, at least she hadn't had to lift the heavy thing off the belt. All she had to do now was get it through the terminal and over to a taxi.

She scanned the crowd, looking for Georgia, but there was no sign of her, or even Kyle, sent in her place. No luck phoning her, either. Each of Noelle's five calls went straight to voicemail.

The taxi lineup was a nightmare. Earlier, when she'd pulled her heavy suitcase past the row of drivers holding up signs with the names of their clients, she'd wished that Georgia and Kyle had offered to spring for a private ride into the city, but she almost instantly gave herself a mental finger-wagging. She knew, from some of Georgia's accounts of their business travels, that ever since their company had been taken over by a multinational, her daughter- and son-in-law usually avoided taxis, shuttle buses, and rental cars, but it was too much to expect that for a personal trip for someone's mother.

Noelle pulled her coat collar up higher around her neck, getting ready to join the crowd on the sidewalk, lined up just outside the door.

The cabs stood at the curb, trunk lids raised and ready for the suitcases, bags, and boxes of gifts.

First, she'd have to do her time in the inside lineup. It snaked back and forth about six times—there were probably three hundred people waiting. Noelle sighed and pulled her bag over to take her place behind them all.

She noticed a tall man in a slate gray top coat that matched his hair approaching people who were waiting in the line about ten feet ahead of her. A cameraman with professional gear followed him.

When she saw him stretch a hand holding a microphone toward a family group of two adults and two kids, she realized it was a TV news crew—the last thing she wanted to see. Noelle turned away so that they wouldn't approach her.

The woman behind her in the lineup was wearing a black puffy jacket, black leggings, a black scarf, boots, and gloves.

"Looks heavy," she commented, looking at Noelle's suitcase. "Full of gifts?"

Noelle grinned. "Of course. For the grandkids."

"Tis the season." The woman pushed her rollaboard forward with her toe as they inched along toward the taxi stand. "You ready?"

"Except for one item. They want something called a mini-GPT3 and I haven't been able to find them anywhere."

Her fellow traveler winced. "Good luck with that."

"I know, right?" Noelle gave her bag a tug. "I was hoping that it might be easier in New York—"

The woman shook her head. "It's not."

The sliding doors to the sidewalk opened in front of them and a blast of cold air pushed its way into the terminal. A driver motioned to Noelle, and she dragged her bag off toward his cab.

It seemed impossible, but the sidewalk was even busier than the terminal itself. The air seemed difficult to breathe and the clouds hung low. Those were clouds full of snow, she could tell.

Whose brilliant idea was it to have Christmas in December? Yes, it was nice to have something to brighten up the dark evenings with lights, parties, shopping, and gifts. But wouldn't it all be so much easier to take care of in July, with the warm air and the long evenings?

Winter was not Noelle's favorite season.

She dragged the suitcase over a small pile of icy snow that someone hadn't noticed when the sidewalk was cleared. It wasn't far to the cab that the attendant signaled she was to claim, but the crowds of people made it slow going.

It was all even more complicated because of a clump of people that had stopped completely, about six feet in front of her taxi. They were surrounding the TV man she'd seen inside.

"Excuse me?" He was coming right at her, with a camera man carrying an enormous piece of equipment labeled Channel 45 right behind him.

Great.

Noelle put on her most annoyed, 'do not bother me' expression, and kept walking.

"Excuse me, would you stop for just a moment? I'm Dan Keyes from Channel 45 News and I'm just talking to folks about coming to New York for the holiday season."

"Well, I guess you're in the right place for it," Noelle said, as she tried to continue moving toward her cab without bumping her suitcase or her bag into anybody.

"Yes, I guess I am, aren't I?" She couldn't tell whether he was just trying to be friendly, to get his job done, or whether there was a bit of humor under his words.

"Are you here on your own?" He was looking over her shoulder, trying to spot an inconsiderate husband bringing up the rear, perhaps.

"Yes, that's my cab." Noelle waved again at her driver, but so far, he was unresponsive.

"No one meeting you then?" Dan the TV man said hopefully.

Noelle stopped in her tracks and made full eye contact with him. "No. No one. No pack of adult children, no gang of cute grandchildren. I'm sorry to dis-appoint you, but there's no story here. You'll have to try someone else for your 'man in the street' interview. Or, woman at the airport, I should say."

"I'm working on a feature about the most wonderful

time of the year," Dan said. "In the most wonderful city. Are you seeing family here?" He didn't wait for Noelle's reply. "We can include everybody in the piece, if you want. If they want."

"No."

Dan the TV man wasn't the least bit rattled by her tone. "That's too bad. I would have liked an excuse to talk with you a little longer.'

"You didn't talk with me at all," Noelle said.

"We could, though," he persisted. "We could talk about Christmas, about the festive season, about family time, about shopping, anything you want."

"I want to get in this cab," Noelle said as, blessedly, the taxi driver appeared in front of her, reaching for her bag. Her mind filled in "you . . .", then a couple of adjectives and nasty names.

The driver took the suitcase from her and heaved it into the trunk. "Good luck with your story."

Dan Keyes reached in front of her and took charge of the handle, opening the back seat door for her. Noelle softened a bit; good manners and a little chivalry went a long way with her. She didn't think she'd seen any since about 1985.

"Thank you very much," she said, as graciously as she could. "Look, I didn't mean to be rude, but I don't want to be on camera and I'm just worn out from the flight."

"I understand," Dan said. "I don't want to bug you or get in your way. Most people are thrilled to be asked, though, so I guess I just didn't pick up on it, that you were trying to dodge me."

"I'm not most people."

"Clearly, not," he said. The eye contact was definitely direct. What was he trying to communicate to her?

Noelle folded herself into the back of the cab. "Atlas March Royal Hotel, please," she said to the driver.

Dan still had not closed the door. Noelle reached for the handle, after mentally kicking herself for saying the name of her hotel out loud. She tugged on the door but Dan was holding it open. "I hope you enjoy your stay in New York," he said. "I really would like to put you in my story about out-of-towners and the festive season—"

"And I really wouldn't want to be there." Noelle smiled to take the edge off her words. "I have to go, Mr. . . . ?"

"Keyes. Dan," he said, reaching toward her with a business card in his left hand, while his right continued to clutch the outside handle of the taxi's back door. "Please call me if you change your mind."

"Come on, buddy, we gotta go." The cab driver had run out of patience.

The taxi had rolled forward, just a few inches, but Noelle had a sudden giddy image of the yellow cab dragging a TV reporter along behind.

She took the card. "All right, Mr. Keyes, thank you. Let go, now. We have to make room for the other cabs behind us." She made a firm yank on the door handle and felt it come toward her, then heard it click into place.

As she watched through the back window, she saw Dan straighten up and give her a wide smile.

She'd have to tell Yvonne and Isabel about this. He was even better looking in person than on TV.

CHAPTER 4

Tucked into the back of the cab and looking up occasionally to take in the passing landscape of concrete freeways and weathered brick buildings in the distance, Noelle took out her phone and scrolled through her camera roll.

Kelsey, with her sweet four-year-old face and halo of fine, red hair; Ken-neth, with his six-year-old body constantly dressed in his superhero costume choice of the week or month; and their younger cousin, Frost, at two years old, already a master of the enchanting smile.

They were on her mind far more often than a handsome TV guy who showed up on her screen from time to time when she watched the news.

But she had to admit to herself that it had been a kick to see him in real life, at the airport, of all places. It would make a good story.

She was happy to be bringing the grandkids the daily cookie feast, but she really wanted to make the holiday truly memorable by handing them each one of those mini-GPT3s.

Frost hadn't asked for one, and he'd probably be happy with anything he received, as long as it came in a cardboard box he could play in. But if the mini-GPT3 was the toy of the season, and she came up with one for each of Georgia's kids, then she'd better not leave Frost out. Daisy would pitch a fit. Probably as big as the one she pitched anytime anybody affectionately added a 'y' to her son's name.

Noelle figured she would go shopping tomorrow, buy three toy robots, and then put one on an express overnight delivery to Portland for Frost.

It was New York, after all. They had everything here, in the city that never sleeps, and she was confident she'd find the toy. The toy to make the holiday truly memorable. To a two-year-old or a four-year-old. Yeah, right?

Noelle had seen the photos of the mini-GPT3 online and she didn't understand what was so special about this doll/action/hero/robot thing. But she wasn't buying one for herself; it was for the kids.

The two older ones had told her on the phone what they wanted. You don't give a skateboarder a football or a science nerd a bell from Santa's sleigh. You want to try to help make a dream come true, for a child at Christmas.

Bracing herself against the bumpy ride, she checked her text messages. Still nothing from Georgia. She decided to connect with her friends.

To Yvonne: *Made it to NYC. How r u?*
To Isabel: *Hi! How was yoga this morning?*

After five more minutes of swerving back and forth to avoid the potholes on the freeway and then bumping through a dozen of them, she even tried Sherry:

Ahoy there!

Instantly, she received a photo of Sherry's hand, nails manicured in a tropical shade of orange, holding a tall drink glass decorated with a tiny umbrella.

None of them needed her, Noelle knew that. They were good friends, but they didn't need her, not in the way that she often needed them. But maybe that would change as they all got older.

Meanwhile, she had her family. What more could she possibly want?

She brought up Georgia's number once more and tried one more text.

I'm in a taxi and I'll see you at the hotel.

This taxicab was not one of New York's finest. It had not been cleaned since the '70s, she would swear, and had only been equipped with shock absorbers shortly before that.

"How much farther to the Atlas March Royal Hotel?"

"Just another half hour," the driver said. He had one eye on the road and one on the GPS screen mounted on his dashboard. She suspected he was also watching another screen, on a phone lying somewhere on the front seat.

Dear God. Would she even survive this ride to get there? Noelle dug through her purse for earbuds, then put them in and turned on the music app on her phone. Frank Sinatra's voice took her away.

As they jolted along, the taxi speeding at what she was sure was twice the limit, she watched the buildings zip by. She was so familiar with this city, from so many movies and TV shows, and she felt as though she'd been here many times. But the visuals weren't syncing with the feeling. It all just seemed rather dreary. The longest half hour ever.

The snow was coming down now, though, and the glistening white stuff was making things look a bit better. But the driver's speed wasn't changing at all, and after they skidded slightly for a third time, Noelle felt she had to speak up.

"Could you slow down a bit, please?"

His response was to step on the accelerator. At least, she thought she felt the cab speed up. They passed a minivan and another taxi on the right. Noelle pulled her coat collar up around her ears and hunkered down with Frank.

The traffic once they reached Manhattan was epic. For a while, Noelle entertained herself by trying to spot a vehicle that wasn't either a yellow cab or a delivery truck.

Third Avenue was stop-and-go, and Forty-second Street was almost a parking lot. Well, so what? She didn't have a deadline for anything and she had never adopted that "my time is valuable, too, you know" attitude. Watching the people go by (some of them walking faster than this cab was moving) was enjoyable, and so was reading the storefront and building signs.

She couldn't see much of the famous New York skyscrapers from the cab, but she knew she'd have plenty of opportunity for that with Georgia and Kyle and the kids.

"How much farther is it to the hotel?" Noelle asked the driver.

"About half an hour," he said. Was that his standard answer for distance questions?

She heard quite a few sirens as they crawled along, but it seemed as though one in particular was becoming more persistent and louder.

After another ten minutes of crawling, and then sitting at a corner for a full five minutes, the driver said, "Let's try something else," and cranked the steering wheel over to turn right.

The siren was instantly louder and in about half a block, Noelle could see the source of the sound. Three firetrucks were parked along the curb beside the Christmas tree in front of Rockefeller Center. The taxi slowed to a crawl, then a stop. A few dozen people stood on the sidewalk, staring up at the tree. Noelle could see no sign of a fire, an accident, or any kind of crime.

"What's going on?" she asked.

"Hard to tell." The driver sounded disgusted.

Noelle pressed the button on the door to roll down the window. "Hey, what's happening?"

"It's a cat," someone said.

A cat? Up the only tree in this part of Manhattan? Noelle had a moment of sympathy for some pet owner who must be having a stressful December Saturday afternoon.

Squinting across the pavement, between all of the bystanders, Noelle caught glimpses of a woman in a black coat, with bare legs in a man's boots, standing beside the ladder, staring up at the firefighter. He was staring up at what might be a cat. Paralyzed by fear, cold, or contrariness. Just out of reach.

"Lady, close the window," the driver demanded.

The traffic moved on and Noelle knew she was doomed to wonder, during her entire week in New York, what had happened to the stuck cat.

**

The hotel was every bit as luxurious as Georgia had promised. Covering an entire city block on the Upper West Side, the Atlas March Royal Hotel was so grand that Noelle felt like the country mouse come to the big city.

She handed over her credit card to the driver, then waited for him to come around to her door. He didn't budge from the front seat, though. Just popped the trunk and waited for her to get herself out of the back seat and her enormous suitcase out onto the side-walk.

Never mind. Noelle didn't give him another thought after the doorman quickly took charge, then handed her suit-case over to the bellhop, who guided her toward the entrance. She walked through the revolving door and into the lobby, coming to a full stop for a few minutes just to absorb the sights around her.

Huge round marble pillars rose two stories to a vaulted ceiling. Two grand pianos anchored either end of the space and a twenty-foot-tall Christmas tree dominated the central area, its lights twinkling and bulbs reflecting the blue and sil-ver color scheme.

Noelle counted a dozen leather couches, two dozen

massive floral ar-rangements, and three dozen poinsettias displayed throughout the lobby. Four hallways beckoned, leading to who-knows-what delights—restaurants? shopping? spa?

Noelle was about to begin an exploration when a voice interrupted.

"May I help you find something?" The young man wore a dark blue suit with the hotel's logo on the front pocket. "Are you checking in?"

"Yes, I am, thank you."

"The reception desk is over this way. Let me take your suitcase for you."

This was exactly Georgia's style, this place. She'd had these champagne tastes (often on a beer budget) ever since she was nine years old. If Noelle had been meeting other-daughter Daisy, she'd be in the lobby of something much more suburban and less costly.

Noelle wasn't sure whether it was her own style. It had been many years since she'd spent any time thinking about what her opinions and preferences were.

Way back when, before marriage and children, when she'd had more free hours, she'd read magazines, traveled, bought things for herself. But as the years went by, and both time and money became tight, she got out of the habit of taking note of her own inclinations.

She knew each of her daughters' favorite colors, foods, and songs; her husband's favorite baseball and basketball teams; the family's choices for vacations, winter and summer. But she gradually lost her grip on her own choices about those things, and one day, it just didn't matter.

She used to like to say that when you are a mother,

you are actually living multiple lives. You are not just keeping track of your own schedule, your health, your work, your feelings, your dreams; you also do that for each child, and, if you are close, for your husband, too.

Then, one day, you just disappear.

The Atlas March Royal was a gorgeous hotel, done, objectively speaking, in impeccable taste, but Noelle just didn't know whether it was her taste.

She gave her head a shake, as if she might somehow settle the cloudiness and uncertainty, but she still felt that disconnection. As she followed the hotel staffer over to the reception desk, she checked her phone once more. Still nothing from Yvonne or Isabel. Or Georgia.

The concierge desk was busy, with a long line of guests waiting to ask about show tickets or city transportation. Noelle noticed an entrance to a restaurant, The Five Continents, with a chef standing out in front talking with a tall, young woman wearing a green, sparkling dress and high heels.

Just then, the concierge left the line of people standing at his desk to go over to speak with the chef. Maybe he'd been asked to set up a restaurant reservation?

At the reception desk, she waited behind a handsome couple who might have been in their late eighties, perhaps even nineties. They held hands. The front desk clerk smiled at them as she handed over their room key cards, and they looked as if there were nowhere on earth they'd rather be.

"Merry Christmas," the man said as they passed Noelle, pulling their suitcases and heading toward the elevators.

"Merry Christmas to you, too."

"First time in New York?" the woman asked.

"Oh no, not my first time," Noelle re-plied. "You?"

"Oh, yes." They both beamed as if they'd won the lottery. Maybe they had.

"Where are you from?"

"We live in California."

"And you wouldn't rather be there, in the warm weather and the sunshine, in December?" Noelle looked to see whether the front desk clerk was becoming impatient with them, but she had turned away to answer a phone call.

"Oh, no," the man said. "We've seen that dozens of times."

"Hundreds," his companion offered helpfully, then they both laughed. "Well, maybe not hundreds."

"But dozens," the man said. "When you get old, you want to see something different, once in a while."

"I don't know about that," Noelle smiled. "I find that I like my familiar surroundings."

"Maybe you're not old enough yet, dear," the woman said.

The front desk clerk put down the phone and turned to Noelle. "Checking in?" she asked.

Noelle nodded in farewell to the couple as they headed off toward the elevator and their room. "Moran," she said.

She scanned the lobby while the clerk searched her computer. A musician in black tie was setting up at one of the pianos, opening the keyboard cover and putting music on the stand.

A woman in an evening gown approached him—was it the same one that she'd seen before, outside the restau-rant? Yes, it was. He sat down on the bench and the woman in the green gown stepped up to stand beside him, holding a micro-phone to her lips.

The chords of "The Christmas Song" wafted out from the piano and rose forty feet, toward the ceiling of the magnif-icent lobby. The singer began to tell them about chestnuts, and suddenly, Noelle began to like New York City a lot more.

"Excuse me?"

Noelle turned back toward the front desk clerk.

"I'm sorry," the woman said with an apologetic tone, "but we don't have a reservation under the name 'Moran.'"

CHAPTER 5

Could it be that Noelle was at the wrong hotel? She doubted she'd made that big a mistake.

"It might be that my daughter put my room under her family name," Noelle said. "What do you have for Finch?"

The clerk took her time, looking through her data. "We do have one reservation for 'Finch' but that party has already checked in."

Noelle was at a loss for what to do next, which made it a very good thing that Georgia rushed up to her a moment later.

"Mom! You're here! We were just going to head over to the airport to look for you."

"Of course, I'm here," Noelle said. "Hello, dear, it's good, to see you." She reached over to Georgia for a hug.

The response was absent-minded. "My phone's gone missing, Mom, and we just got off a long conference call on Kyle's phone," Georgia said. "Everybody from the company is coming into town for the meeting, but some of them got messed up by the bad weather. We were trying to sort everybody out, and the call went long, and then I couldn't find my phone. . . I knew we'd be late, but I thought you'd wait for us at the airport!"

"My, my, what did people do before they had a phone to carry around in their pocket?" Noelle said. "Anyway, I'm here now."

"Isn't it a beautiful hotel?"

"Yes, it is, but apparently, I'm not staying here."

"Yes, you are, Mom, but we have you in our suite."

"In your suite!"

"Yes, I thought it would be awesome if we were all in the same place, in a big suite. More homey, more being-to-gether-for-Christmas, rather than down the hall, in another room." Georgia was chattering. "They have a fantastic spa here and a huge swimming pool. We got you a pass for the week."

The reservations clerk was giving them a tense smile and glancing over their heads at the guests behind them, waiting to sign in. Noelle stepped aside and took a few deep breaths while she thought over this latest development. She could see Georgia's point; it would be nice to have that much time together, a little less like being in a hotel for Christmas.

"Well, all right, Georgia. I'm sure that will be fine," she said. She was used to having a lot more space than that, and a lot more time to herself. But this fresh development shouldn't put her off. Wasn't that lack of company exactly what had been getting to her? Hadn't she been yearning for more family time? So, now she was going to get some.

"There's another thing, Mom. I was wondering . . . Kyle and I were won-dering . . . if you could help us out this week."

Help you out? It can't be money you need, Noelle thought. Look at the way you're dressed. Look at this hotel. Is it a problem with your boss? With Kyle's mother?

Noelle would give her right arm to help either of her daughters, any time, but she had to admit that this time, especially since she'd just rearranged all her plans to come to New York City on less than a day's notice, she was having trouble guessing what the ask might be.

"With the kids," Georgia said. "It turns out we have a lot of commitments, with the new corporation taking us over and giving us these big titles and so much money and every-thing."

"I thought you were here for their annual Christmas party."

"Yes, there's that. But there's a lot of other meetings, too." Georgia gazed around the lobby, and despite Noelle's intense efforts, avoided any eye contact. "Pretty much all day, every day."

Noelle walked over to one of the leather couches and sat down next to a table covered in a tiny North Pole village. Georgia followed and sat down beside her. "You won't be available to enjoy New York with me this week, then."

"No."

"It's Christmas week and you invited me here but you won't be taking any time off work to do things with me."

"Yes."

"And you want me to babysit."

"Yes."

"Pretty much all day, every day."

"Yes. But I don't think I'd call it "babysitting", Georgia said. "We don't call it babysitting when Kyle is with the kids. They're his kids. They're your grandkids. It's not babysitting, like for pay."

"Uh-huh." Noelle wasn't happy about this, but she wasn't sure why not. She should be delighted to be offered full-time, unlimited access to her grandchildren, shouldn't she? Georgia needed her. That should make her feel great, shouldn't it? And the kiddies would be much better off with her than with a paid stranger, wouldn't they?

"Come on, Mom, let's go up and see the kids and get you settled," Georgia said. She stood up and gave Noelle's suitcase a good pull. "We could have used Kyle down here to carry this thing around, but he's still tied up on the phone."

Noelle trailed along behind Georgia, through the lobby and past the twenty-foot tree. The lovely young woman with the green dress and the jazzy voice was still pouring Christmas carols out into the afternoon. Noelle paused to smile at her and join in the smattering of applause at the end of "I'll Be Home for Christmas."

All the way up on the elevator to the thirty-fifth floor, Noelle did battle with her feelings of guilt. A good mother didn't turn her back on a child when she needed her, did she? It wasn't the grandchildren's fault that all the grownups in their lives were very busy, right around the holidays, was it? Shouldn't she be thrilled to be asked to pitch in?

They stopped at a huge white double door while Georgia fumbled with the key card. She looked stressed, but what working mother wasn't, a week before Christmas?

Georgia pushed open the door and Noelle had to stop for a minute to take it all in. The suite was every bit as impressive as the lobby.

It was decorated in muted neutrals, beige on cream on ivory, with the occasional touch of red and green in a nod to the holiday season.

Georgia walked over to a white velvet couch and sat herself gracefully down. When had she become so chic? Noelle wondered sometimes how she could have given birth to and raised two daughters so different from one another and so different from their mother. Usually, when she drove down to Cincinnati to visit Georgia, she saw her wearing leggings and T-shirts, cleaning up after the little ones or driving in the carpool. Today, she wore a black suit, serious heels, and black chandelier earrings that looked terrific with her red hair.

"Hello, Noelle. How are you? How was your flight?" Kyle's voice entered the room five seconds before he did.

"It was fine, Kyle. It's nice to see you," Noelle said as she settled herself on the couch next to Georgia. "I've just been hearing about your busy week coming up."

Her son-in-law was as well put together as his wife, all the way from his perfectly pressed shirt to his brown shoes. Everything looked brand new.

"Yes, it's just crazy! Ever since we sold our toy company to those guys, they've had us running full-speed. And of course, Christmas time, that's our biggest time of year," he said, helping himself to some snacks on a plate on the glass-topped coffee table. "After summer holidays and Black Friday and spring break, of course."

"Nonny Noelle!" Kenneth launched himself into the room and into her lap. Kelsey was right on his heels.

"Hey, you guys, don't break Nonny Noelle on her very first afternoon here," Kyle said. "You'll have all week to play with her."

"I've been thinking about all this," Noelle said. She could feel Georgia tense up. "I'm going to enjoy spending lots of time with them, but I hadn't really expected to be responsible for them all week. I have a few things yet to shop for, and I'd like to do some sight-seeing on my own, see if I can't get the hang of New York a little more. Do you think maybe your mother could pitch in, too, Kyle? Her place is just a few miles away, isn't it?"

Kyle looked doubtful and Georgia's head gave a brief twitch from right to left, almost as if she couldn't help it. Noelle wasn't surprised; Pamela hadn't really impressed her as the babysitter type. Not the grandmother type, either—if there was such a thing.

Georgia had told Noelle that her mother-in-law had never visited them in Cincinnati. Her time with the kids had increased as they got older, past the infant and toddler stages, and she'd invited them several times for visits to a resort-hotel near a beach. But they were definitely visits, not offers to look after the grandkids.

"I'm sure it will all work out," Georgia said. "Mom, come on, I'll show you where you're sleeping. Kyle, could you please bring in Mom's suitcase?"

"Yeah, okay . . . oh, just a sec, I have to take this," he said, looking down at his buzzing phone and then heading off to a corner of the room where an antique desk commanded a view of the park.

Georgia led Noelle down a hallway and opened a door. "Here it is! I'll leave you for a while to freshen up, maybe take a nap. The kids have had lunch and they're going to have quiet time for a while. I'll put on a movie."

As soon as she was alone, Noelle allowed her jaw to drop. The room was so tiny she suspected it had once been a walk-in closet. Georgia had seemed so thrilled with the idea that they would all stay in the same suite . . . but was she, really?

Noelle was suspicious now that everything, her entire trip, the room in the suite, the special pass to the pool, all had to do with the convenience of having Nonny Noelle babysit.

Her phone lit up with a text. Yvonne.

All good here, how r u?

Not what Noelle would call a tidal wave of girlfriend attention, especially when Yvonne knew every detail of her di-emma over whether to go on this visit to New York at all.

But what could you expect? Yvonne had Sam and her bakery to keep her busy. Noelle had had little to do since she'd retired from her school teacher job. It seemed like a good idea at the time, especially because her students appeared more like exotic jungle beasts instead of humans to her now. But it left her with no work, no husband, and no kids nearby. Oh, sure, she had yoga classes, sewing, book club, and redecorating her kitchen. But that wasn't actually "busy".

Her phone buzzed again with a new message, this one from Sherry. That was six, in the past two hours. Photos of the ship's pool, the view from the top deck, her cabin, the shops, and one of the bars. Noelle didn't think she wanted to make travel her retirement hobby but if she did, Sherry would be right there, ready to be her geography buddy.

She texted back an enthusiastic emoji, a jaw-dropper, and two thumbs-up. In a little while, she'd be out in the New York streets and she'd have a few of her own.

Georgia had Kelsey and Kenneth ready to go the minute that Noelle emerged from her room/closet.

"They're so excited to get out into the city and see some of the Christmas decorations, Mom!" Georgia said, as she tied a scarf around Kenneth's throat.

"We want to watch cartoons!" Kenneth pulled at his scarf and tried to untie it.

"Toons!" echoed Kelsey.

"We could do that," Noelle said. "We could cuddle up right here on the couch and watch some shows together, maybe see what Nonny brought in one of the tins in her suitcase?"

"The thing is, Noelle, we have a meeting happening here in about half an hour and we need to use the room," Kyle said. "If you could take the kids out for a few hours, it would be a big help."

Well, that's just great.

This was the time of day when she often grabbed a nap, and Noelle felt a tide of sleepiness rise up around her. After the drive to the Burlington airport, the flight, the taxi ride and a half hour with Georgia, she needed a rest more than usual.

But she gave herself a shake: what was she thinking? It was Christmas. She had her two grandchildren there, and she was needed. She headed for the closet to retrieve her coat.

"Yes, of course. We're on our way. Come on, you two. Let's go see some New York."

CHAPTER 6

So now, she had walked Fifth Avenue with her grandchildren and taken them to the biggest Santa workshop in the city. And she'd managed to lose one of them. She had to be the worst grand-mother of all time.

The worst grandmother, the least popular mother, and the only woman in the northeast without someone special at Christmas.

If Noelle hadn't promised those cookies to the little ones, she would have pulled up the covers on her bed here in this closet and eaten half a dozen from each tin herself.

A few minutes later, when her phone lit up with an unfamiliar number, Noelle almost ignored it. It was probably somebody wanting to sell her something. Where did these people get cell phone numbers, anyway?

But something prompted her to tap the green button and say hello.

"Ms. Moran? Noelle?"

It was a pleasant voice, but it was nobody she knew,

so he'd better hurry up and introduce himself or he'd be dumped by delete button.

"This is Matt Kezanski. From the store yesterday?"

Well, my, my. Noelle didn't know what to say.

"Ma'am? Are you still there?"

"Yes, I'm here." Noelle sat down on the bed. "I think I remember you, Mr. Kezanski. But I won't be on the phone for long, if you keep on calling me ma'am."

"We met at Santa's Workshop in the Toy Department."

Tactful of him not to say "when you misplaced your four-year-old granddaughter, leaving her at the mercy of whatever lunatic or kidnapper might hang out between the building blocks and the craft kits".

"Yes, Mr. Kezanski. How are you?"

He skipped past the small talk and got right to the heart of things. "You seemed very upset, even after we got her back, and I wanted to make sure you're okay."

"Thank you."

"Thank you, Ms. Moran. Noelle. May I call you Noelle?"

"As long as you promise not to make any lame Christmas jokes."

"I guess you've heard them all." Matt cleared his throat. "Are you sure everything is okay now? I hope you're not beating yourself up over what happened."

"Well, I am, Mr. Kezanski."

"Matt."

"Matt. A good grandmother doesn't misplace a four-year-old."

"Unless that four-year-old has the personality of Anne of Green Gables and the escape skills of Harry Houdini."

Noelle thought about it for a long moment, then laughed. "Yes, she is one of a kind. And I have to say, I appreciate being able to talk about it with someone like you. Most people wouldn't be able to make the Houdini reference."

"Most people not in our vintage age group, you mean?"

Noelle laughed, giving him permission to continue.

"Am I correct in guessing that you're not from New York?"

"Vermont. Burlington."

"Have you been to New York before?"

"Only once. A long time ago."

"Only once! That's hard to believe."

"As a New Yorker, Matt, you might find it hard to believe, but many people don't want to spend any time here. And Vermont has a lot going for it."

"Such as?"

"Such as beautiful scenery. Maple syrup. Covered bridges. Lakes. Lake Champlain." Noelle stopped to think. "Cows."

"Cows, yes, okay, cows. Anything else, Noelle? Or do you stay in Vermont and don't even go down the road a little way to New York because you've lived there your whole life and your horizon is pretty close in?"

"I have lived there my whole life, yes." Why did Noelle feel defensive? "I like it there. My family is there."

"Are they?"

"Well, they come back to visit."

"But here you are in New York. At Christmas time."

"Yes, New York, where the streets are in such terrible shape that you could break a hip if the cab driver goes over a pothole too fast!"

They were both laughing. "Yeah, well, Vermont has blizzards and tons of snow," Matt said.

"So do you! Look at it, out there." Noelle had no window, but she was quite sure that the snowfall wasn't over yet.

"It's very pretty, I think," Matt said. "You know what's even prettier? And is one of New York's best spots? The skating rink in Central Park."

Noelle's phone buzzed with an incoming call. What did she do now? Could she put him on hold somehow and check on this unknown number? What if it was Sherry, with some sort of crisis on the ship?

"Just a moment, Mr.—" What was his last name again? "Matt, I have another call coming in."

The print on the screen was too small to read, but she connected the call anyway. "Sherry? Is that you?"

"Why no, Ms. Moran, this is Dan Keyes from Channel 45. You remember, we met yesterday in the Toy Department? At Santa's Workshop? I'm just calling to make sure the little girl is all right, and that you got back to your hotel okay."

"Thank you, Mr. Keyes, yes, we're all fine."

There was a long pause. Obviously, this wasn't really the reason for his call. "I'm interested in doing a feature on grandmas, grandpas, and grandkids, exploring New York over the holidays, highlights, excursions, concerts, sightseeing, that kind of thing, you know?"

Noelle couldn't think of anything she would rather do less.

"No, thank you, Mr. Keyes, but no, I don't think we'd be interested in anything like that." There was silence at the other end; Noelle could feel that he was getting ready to try to be persuasive. "I don't think your viewers would find us very interesting either."

"Oh, I think you're quite wrong about that. I've been working on holiday features all week and the response from the viewers has been incredibly positive. It's that time of year, you know? Ever since Thanksgiving, we've been showing hours of material about families together, enjoying themselves and each other, and the viewers just eat it up. Did you see my item last night?"

She hated to lie, but she really didn't want to discuss it with him. Ignore the question: that would work. "Well, Mr. Keyes, I'll think about it. But we're very busy this week—"

"I think you might find out it's a lot of fun, to see New York this way."

She had a flash of a memory of his broad shoulders in a gray topcoat and his handsome face. Maybe. . .

Her phone buzzed. "I'm sorry, but I have another call."

"That's all right, Ms. Moran, I have to go, too. We'll be in touch."

She tapped at a green button on the phone screen. "Hello?"

"Oh. Noelle. I thought we'd been cut off." Matt's voice sounded anxious.

Noelle could hear Georgia's voice calling from the living room. "I finished my other call, Mr. Kezanski, but now I have to go. It was very kind of you to call to check on us."

"Please. Call me Matt. And I'm phoning to do more than check on you," he said. "In my official capacity as New York City promotions volunteer, I'd like to show you a few of the highlights of my town, maybe give you some ideas of places to take your grandkids. I think you should come over to the rink at Central Park, meet me for a coffee, and we'll discuss it."

"Oh, so now you're bored with security work and you've become a tour guide?" Noelle was more than a little shocked at herself for saying that.

He laughed. "I think I'll be very good at it. Call me back and let me know." And he was gone.

Noelle found Georgia at the dining room table with papers, file folders, two laptop computers, and two phones spread around her. Kelsey and Kenneth were on the couch, watching TV.

"Oh, Mom, good, you're up and around. We're just swamped. I have thirty-four emails I have to answer, and Kyle is already on a conference call. I'd like to be able to take a break for lunch, but I won't know for a few hours. What do you have planned for the kids?"

"Good morning, Georgia. Nothing yet. I haven't even had coffee," she said, looking around the dining room. There was a coffee-maker on a shelf, but it was empty.

"We've been up for hours and we finished the first pot already. You can make another one, though. There's extra packages of coffee there, I think. Or we could call Room Service, if you want breakfast?" Georgia's attention had been reclaimed by her computer and she chatted while she read her screen and typed.

"Great, I'll do that," Noelle said.   "Make the coffee, I mean. I don't need Room Service. I think there's a café in the lobby and I can pop down there for breakfast later."

She stood by Georgia's chair silently for a few minutes until her daughter looked up. "I will think up some activities for the kiddies for later but I might have to go out for a while."

"Oh, Mom, really? Not for long, I hope? What is it, some shopping you need to do? We can send out for anything you need."

"I will not delegate my Christmas shopping to anybody else, Georgia, come on." Noelle backed away from the table. She needed some space. "I'm going to go downstairs to get a bagel and some coffee. I'll be back in half an hour."

The lobby was a private place to have a conversation, and as soon as she had tucked herself into an elegant burgundy velvet armchair beside one of the Christmas trees, she pulled out her phone to call Yvonne.

A commotion just behind the grand piano on the other side of the alcove grabbed her attention.

"The jazz brunch doesn't start for another three hours, Harmonie! You have plenty of time to pitch in and give us a hand. It's not as if they're asking us to clear tables or clean rooms!"

"Donald, look at this place! It's overdone with lights and crap already!"

Noelle leaned over in the chair to get a better look at them. The man barely reached the tall woman's shoulder. He was dressed in a hotel uniform that didn't fit very well and his beard could have used some attention.

The woman had long hair and perfect posture—wait a minute! It was the one Noelle had seen with the chef outside the restaurant when she was trying to check in at the desk yesterday and then had seen later, singing Christmas carols with the pianist in the lobby.

As she stared at them, she realized that the man was the concierge she'd seen on duty yesterday afternoon.

"Come on, it'll be fun. They're understaffed in the Sales and Events department and they really need some help to get set up for this big family group that's booked in for dinner after the ballet matinée."

"I don't do party set up or holiday decorating, Donald. I'm a singer. I'm the singer, that's what I do. I'm just here a little early today but I'm busy until the show starts at eleven."

Maybe Noelle's interest had become so intense that they could feel it across the lobby. Harmonie suddenly looked over, made eye contact with Noelle, then discreetly pointed her out to Donald.

They both nodded at her and then walked away toward the reception desk.

Noelle picked up her phone to call Yvonne. Thirty seconds into the conversation, after she summarized her meeting yesterday with Matt and his invitation this morning, Yvonne delivered her opinion.

"So, what's the problem?" her friend asked. "You met a good-looking guy. He asked you on a date. Go."

"It's a little more complicated than that," Noelle said. "I haven't been out with a man since Ian passed away. And I don't know that we'd call this invitation to have a coffee a date."

"Near a very romantic place in a very exciting city?"

"You're hallucinating," Noelle said. "Besides, I've got Georgia expecting me to look after the grandkids today."

"All day long?"

"Well, I did tell her I had something I needed to go out to do. And I do have some last-minute shopping. But I worry about them. What will they do, if I'm not there? Georgia will leave them to watch TV all day while she does her work. Or, she might stop working to look after them and then what if there's some royal screw-up at the company?"

"Not your issue. What do you think they do when you're not there?"

"Well, I know, they get along fine, because they have to. But when I'm right here, and I can pitch in and help, I want to!"

"And you are helping. But they've had lots of your attention already and you don't have to be the full-time nanny or their second mom to show them love."

Noelle munched on her poppyseed bagel and tried to understand her own feelings about this. She didn't want to be pushed into going on a date just because Yvonne thought she should. But she also didn't want to let Georgia run her life.

"Besides," Yvonne said, working up a head of steam, "will grandkids keep you warm at night? No, they won't. And that's important, Noelle."

"Not at my age, it's not."

"Yes, it is." It was rare for Yvonne to be so argumentative, but perhaps Noelle rarely offered an opportunity like this, giving Yvonne something to push back against. "You're not ninety."

"Even ninety-year-olds need love!" Noelle heard Sam's baritone in the background. Apparently, her social life was up for public discussion with her friends' husbands.

But she really shouldn't be so sarcastic, even silently. Yvonne and Sam were a package deal. She knew that. It was part of what made Yvonne, Yvonne.

But if Yvonne could push back, so could she. "But I'm not on this trip to meet guys. It's Christmas week, for heaven's sake. It's about family, not men."

"Of course, Noelle, I'm not arguing that. I'm just saying, take a few hours for yourself. Go have coffee in Central Park and have a chat with a new friend. That's all."

She's right, Noelle thought. Why imagine it into something so complicated?

Yvonne wasn't done. "Don't forget how hard you've worked for your kids already. The shopping, the late nights wrapping gifts, the cooking, the cleaning, the baking, the parties. Taking them to see Santa year after year, helping them make dreams and add some magic to life. All with no help from Ian, who worked so hard at the office that he'd show up at home at eight on Christmas Eve, with a whole new set of plans and supplies for the holiday that he'd never bothered to discuss with you. You're due some 'me' time, Noelle. That's my opinion."

After she and Yvonne disconnected, Noelle still wasn't ready to return to the suite. She went back to the café takeout window to order her second cup. A lineup had formed while she was on the phone; about a dozen people now stood waiting. Was there somewhere else to get a coffee?

Noelle glanced toward the open door to the lounge and saw some activity inside. Half a dozen people sat in the dim light, about three or four to a table. They all had glasses or coffee cups in front of them.

"Excuse me? I was just wondering whether you're open for breakfast? Or just coffee, that's all I want, actually."

The man behind the bar smiled. "We're not really open, except for staff. But sure, we can do that. Long lineup at the coffee shop?"

"It's a zoo," Noelle said.

"Just help yourself," the bartender said, nodding toward the pot at the end of the bar.

A woman was just ahead of Noelle, pouring herself a cup, and when she turned around, Noelle realized it was Harmonie, the singer who'd been arguing with the concierge out in the lobby.

"Hello," Harmonie said, holding out the pot to pour for Noelle. "I recognize you from the lobby. I hope we didn't disturb you. It was just a minor dispute over work responsibilities."

"Not at all," Noelle answered. Something about this girl's friendly smile and happy eyes made Noelle glad that she'd stepped into this room. It was always a lovely feeling when you clicked right away. "Did you work it out?"

"I think so. At least, they know not to expect me to show up to hang garland in Banquet Room B. I've got a performance coming up."

"Do you need time to prepare?"

"Oh no, it's not that. I'm ready to sing, and we had rehearsal yesterday. We always do, the day before the Sunday Jazz Brunch. It was a long one, too. It takes a while to brush up on all those Christmas songs. No, it's just that I knew that setting up a banquet room would put me in such a bad mood that I wouldn't be able to do my best job on stage for the rest of the week. Especially if I had to do it alongside Donald." Harmonie smiled. "Are you enjoying your stay at our hotel?"

Noelle smiled back. "Oh yes, it's a beautiful place. I'm here visiting with my daughter and her family."

"Are you getting out to sightsee in the city?"

"In a little while, yes. In fact, I'm thinking of heading over to Central Park to see the skaters soon. What's the best way to get there?"

"It's walking distance . . . although with the snow coming down, you might want to take a cab. We can get you one right outside the entrance," Harmonie sipped at her coffee. "But why are you going on your own?"

"I'm going over to meet someone there." When had she decided that? "Or, I might be."

Harmonie tilted her head with a smile, curiosity written all over her face.

"I met a guy yesterday in a department store," Noelle said. Something about Harmonie made her feel like confiding. "He seemed very nice, but I don't know, what do you think? I mean, this is a big city, he's a stranger. What would you do?"

"Say yes!" No hesitation from Harmonie. "I try to always say yes, unless it's illegal or dangerous. And it depends what kind of dangerous. Does it feel dangerous? Does it give you a queasy feeling in your gut? Then, don't go. But if there were no bad signals, then go. To a big public place with lots of people, like the skating rink? On a Sunday morning? I'd say, go. Then, you just plan to leave if there's anything you don't like." She lifted her chin to speak to someone behind Noelle's shoulder. "What do you say, chef?"

Noelle turned around. The young man in the white chef's jacket was the same one she'd seen outside the restaurant when she'd tried to check in. "I agree. Always trust your gut." He smiled at Noelle, but he wasn't really seeing her. His gaze was on Harmonie. "In all things. Especially in choices for breakfast, lunch, or dinner. Appetizers, soups, salads, entrées, or desserts."

"Vegetables, protein, carbs, or wine," Harmonie carried on. "All right then, it's a green light for Miss . . ."

She paused, and Noelle supplied her name. "Noelle."

"Such a pretty name!" Harmonie said. "Miss Noelle. And I am Harmonie Randolph, and this is Justin Paul, our hotel chef."

"I'm looking forward to sampling some of your meals while we're here," Noelle said.

"You should definitely book in for our Christmas Eve Dickens Buffet, if you haven't already done that," Justin said. "We do four sittings throughout the day, brunch, lunch, dinner, and late evening. It's super-popular but there might be a few tickets left."

"I'll look into that," Noelle said, then took a last sip. "Thank you for the coffee, Miss Harmonie."

"And you have two votes in favor of going over to the skating rink at Central Park," Harmonie said. "For another coffee."

"That makes three," Noelle said.

On her way across the lobby toward the elevator, her phone buzzed. Sherry's number and photo appeared on the screen. A few minutes and questions later, she had a fourth vote in favor of meeting Matt at the park.

Would it be unanimous?

Not as far as Georgia was concerned. She followed Noelle, step for step, through the suite. "Going out today? What do you mean?"

"I mean, I'm going for a walk. Going to do some shopping, see some of the city." She couldn't stop moving around, straightening things, and putting away toys. She decided against mentioning Matt's invitation or asking for Georgia's opinion about meeting him. A walk and some shopping seemed controversial enough.

"But it would be such a help if you were here and the kids could go to you if they need something," Georgia said. "We can put on a video. I promise, it will be a quiet day."

"Georgia, I really have to get this shopping done."

"Mom, why didn't you have that all done before you came, anyway? You're usually so organized for Christmas."

"Well, I didn't know that I'd be coming to New York until yesterday, did I? And I didn't know you'd be so busy with work that you'd be expecting me to be with the kiddies full time! And how am I supposed to shop for them if they're with me every minute?" She could feel herself getting upset; really, she should have a lot more self-control than this.

Noelle watched Georgia struggle for her own self-control. "But Kyle won't——" She took a deep breath. "You're right, Mom, of course. We'll manage. When do you think you'll be back?"

Noelle looked past her toward the couch, where Kenneth and Kelsey sat, watching cartoons. It would be so much easier to stay here.

CHAPTER 7

The Park was beautiful, even in its winter mood. Noelle had seen so many movies featuring Central Park, and she thought it might be difficult to see it with fresh eyes.

But she was wrong. The new snow was piled up along the sides of the paths and the bare trees looked like thin ink lines on a sketch. The people she passed were out walking dogs, jogging for exercise, or strolling along, looking at the views, nature on one side and the mind-blowing New York City skyline on the other.

There was a sense of Christmas in the air that had nothing to do with the chestnuts roasting on sidewalk carts or the freshly cut evergreen trees stacked up in a temporary lot on the corner. It wasn't a scent; it was a spirit.

But maybe she was imagining it.

Twenty minutes later, when Noelle was tucked in at a metal table for two with Matt at a café overlooking the ice-skating rink, that Christmas vibe was even stronger.

She ordered a gingerbread cookie to go with her peppermint latté and though it wasn't anywhere near as tasty as the one baked by whoever that was at the cookie swap back home, it was still on the list as an epic cookie. She would have bought a couple to take home to the kids, but if there was one thing she wasn't in any need of, it was extra gingerbread cookies. A dozen of them sat in a tin in her suitcase back at the hotel.

She was holding those for Christmas Eve. This morning, she'd pulled out the red tin with the sugar cookies and shortbread out right after breakfast.

Georgia hadn't been thrilled but backed off when Noelle explained that's what grandmas were for, not for teaching about nutrition or making rules. Maybe her daughter was worried that Noelle would wander out to go shopping that Sunday morning and never return if the babysitting demands irritated her enough. Georgia wanted Noelle's help on Monday, probably for a full twelve or fourteen hours, she said.

"Didn't I tell you it's a pretty sight?" Matt warmed his hands on his own mug of coffee as they sat and watched the skaters go by.

"All right, I surrender," Noelle said, pulling her coat collar up around her ears. Her scarf was back at the hotel, somewhere in the suitcase she hadn't unpacked because there was no room to store her clothes. "This is a good part of New York . . . and I do admit now that there are some. Maybe one or two."

"Ouch!" He smiled at her and she felt her insides turn over a little bit. Why do they call it a 'killer smile'? Whatever that meant, he certainly had one. "You know, it would be even

80

better if we were out there, with them."

"You mean, skating? I haven't skated in thirty years."

"Living in Vermont? Excuse me, ma'am. Where it's icy and snowy for eight months of the year?"

"It is not! You don't know what you're talking about!" Noelle was enjoying herself. "And that's enough calling me 'ma'am'. Where does that come from, anyway? Are you from the south? Or the old west?"

He laughed. "Alright, you're right. I don't really know why I call certain women by 'ma'am' but I'll stop if you want me to. Now, let's get back to the main point. How about we rent some skates and get out there?"

Noelle sipped her coffee, then shook her head. "No, thanks."

Over the years, she'd learned how to shut down discussion on something she didn't want to do and her firm tone of voice usually worked with people. Not with Matt.

"Come on. You know you'll regret it later tonight when you're thinking back over the day."

Noelle stared out at the rink full of skaters: the little girl with the blue hat, clutching her daddy's hands and trying to learn to skate backwards; the couple arm-in-arm and racing past everyone else; the woman in the middle of the crowd, spinning as if she were in a world all of her own.

Then she saw an older couple, a little bent over, a lot slower than anyone else on the rink. He wore a dark green coat that looked as if it might have been military issue, once upon a time. She had on blue jeans and a sheepskin coat, with a long black scarf that reached past her knees. She was clutching his hand for balance, but there was no fear or even mild uneasiness on either of their faces. They were both laughing.

That was it—Noelle was in.

Every minute of it was awkward but she just had to giggle at how silly she was sure she looked . . . and then, it was fine. Her feet started to hurt within the first five minutes and if her knees could speak, they'd be yelling at her: Are you kidding me?!

It was all over-the-top difficult; she didn't know why she thought she'd be able to step out on the ice in some sort of movietime moment.

Skating was one of those things that she'd tried once or twice, decided wasn't her thing, and found ways to avoid. In her teenage years in the '60s, the boys played hockey and the girls went to watch.

The exceptions were the ones who were figure skaters, but they'd been identified and streamed early, put into pretty, white skates and short velvet skating skirts before middle school.

Noelle had shown no promise in that direction, whenever her mother had pushed the family into a skating outing, and eventually, skating dropped off the table as a winter activity.

Once in a while during college, her social life demanded she join in with skating, but she usually had the arm of a boyfriend or a date to hold her up. Maybe he realized she had zero skating skills or maybe he thought she was playing the helpless female. Either way, she didn't have to skate for long, before hot cocoa or something stronger called them off the ice.

That was all a long time ago. Noelle was old enough now that she didn't do things she didn't want to do and didn't bother with things so new that she'd have to fall on her butt at the beginning. So, what was she doing, jerking around the Central Park rink, her ankles wobbling, leaning on this guy?

It was the opportunity to try it in an iconic place like Central Park, that's what it was.

Noelle bumped along for half an hour, almost getting a wind burn from the accomplished skaters zipping past her. The inspiring vintage couple had disappeared. When her phone buzzed with a text, she was relieved and happy to have a good excuse to find a place off to the side of the crowd to look at her screen.

Dan who? Oh, yes, that TV reporter. What did he want?

Matt was right beside her. "Do you need to take that?"

"Yes, do you mind?"

"Not a bit."

Noelle read the text. "It's that TV reporter from the store yesterday. He wants to do some sort of story about the kiddies."

Matt's killer smile disappeared. "Now?"

"No, tomorrow. I'm not thrilled about the idea, but Georgia is." She tapped at the screen. "I'll just tell him I'll deal with it tomorrow at the hotel."

Matt nodded, then reached out to take her hand. "Let's call it a day here. Could we go for a walk?"

Noelle and Matt walked back through the snow, stopping to look into every second window. A tiny toy store caught Noelle's eye and as she watched the toy train run around a track that circled a miniature North Pole, she remembered that she still hadn't finished her shopping. The grandkids were loving their cookies, but she doubted that would be enough to dazzle them on Christmas morning.

Georgia had mentioned to her that Pamela had some impressive gifts from "other-grandma" ready to go, and even though she knew it was childish, that just got Noelle's competitive juices flowing.

Noelle had met Pamela for the first time on the same day that Georgia did—on the wedding day. Kyle's mother lived an exotic life, part time in New York City and part time in Miami. She'd flown in to Burlington the morning of the wedding and had only stayed over one day.

It wasn't that Noelle had hoped to find a lifelong friend or even expected to spend a lot of time with the other parent of the bridal couple. But she'd been part of the scene when Yvonne's daughter, Sophie, got married, and had watched as Yvonne and Sophie's husband's mom partied until the wee hours of the morning after the wedding dance. It was her only experience of the situation and she'd assumed it was what people did.

Pamela surprised her, that was all. There was nothing negative about it, and it didn't foreshadow trouble coming. She'd stressed that to Yvonne and Isabel when they talked over Georgia's wedding afterward.

Sometimes it was whole families getting married and somehow, she had thought that would be what would happen this time.

Ian was still alive for Georgia's wedding and he had seen nothing strange about Pamela's behavior. So, Noelle just concluded that Pamela surprised her, that was all. Didn't disappoint her, didn't put her off.

Over the next few years, Pamela did scare her a few times, though. She showed up when Kenneth was born and insisted on group family photos when he was only a day old. Noelle thought she could see that Georgia wasn't happy about it, but Georgia insisted it was fine.

Then, when Kelsey was born, she hadn't managed to make the trip, but the day that Georgia arrived home, a baby nurse and a maid showed up at the house. Kyle explained their services were a gift from his mother, and even though Noelle thought that Georgia might have preferred not to have strangers around, but she couldn't really turn down such a generous gift from her mother-in-law, could she?

Now it was Christmas, and Pamela had some amazing gifts for the grandchildren, she was told. Noelle didn't feel that her daughter was urging her on to some sort of toxic, gift-giving competition, but she believed that she had a deep understanding of the two, four, and six-year-old hearts, when it came to presents, and she wanted to thrill Frost, Kelsey, and Kenneth.

Maybe this store would have a mini-GPT3 robot? Or know where she could get one?

"Nice dollhouse," Matt said, looking over an intricate construction with six bedrooms, a library, a gym, an immense kitchen, and a matching kennel. "Is that what you have in mind for Kelsey? Or maybe you've already finished your shopping?"

"I have a few gifts for them, but the big one is this mini-GPT3 robot thing."

"Aren't you going to wait to see whether you won the department store prize?"

"No, if they have one of those toys here, I'm on it. If we win the prize at the store, it'll be a bonus. It's only six days to Christmas. That already feels way too late, to me. Let's ask if they have any."

This toy store was the most elaborate that Noelle had ever seen, even though it was small. Every category of kids' toy and every age group was represented. Maybe she could bring Kenneth and Kelsey over here tomorrow and get some ideas for alternative presents for them, if the robot toy idea didn't pan out.

"What was your favorite toy?" Matt asked, as he watched her pick up a box of wooden train pieces.

"It's hard to remember back that far." Noelle tried to brush off the question, but there was something about his manner that made it hard to do. "All right, let me think. It was a toy oven, and it came with these adorable plastic mixing bowls and spoons and all the trimmings. I was about five. What about you?"

"A doctor's kit, little stethoscope, tongue depressors, the works."

Noelle almost made a joke about playing doctor, but managed to rein it in. Back in the '70s, that would have passed by easily, without comment, but these days it was probably inappropriate.

"What will you get them if you can't find these robots?" he asked.

"I've already bought books for each of them, a doll for Kelsey, cars and a track for Kenneth. Frost, he's two, he's getting a big truck from me. I mainly bought it for the cardboard box. That's what he'll enjoy the most."

Matt laughed, then wandered over to inspect a stack of hats. He lifted a Stetson from the top and placed it on Noelle's head. She tilted her chin and posed, and they were locked on each other for a moment.

What was going on?

Noelle took the hat and put it back with the others, then smiled at Matt. "You know, other than the robots, what I think they want the most is a Christmas tree. Kenneth's been asking, over and over, whether they'll be getting a tree in the room. I think he has it in his head somehow that Santa won't be able to deliver if there isn't a tree there. He's already figured out there isn't such a thing as a chimney in a hotel suite, but I think he thinks that as long as there's a tree, it will work out."

"Did they have one at home?"

Noelle paused in her inspection of a shelf of board games. "You know, I hadn't thought of that, but yes, they did. He's probably missing it."

Matt nodded. "Maybe feels like they abandoned it, in some way. Kids can get funny ideas."

"Do you have children, Matt?"

"I have no children. I did have children but they're all over thirty-five now, so I refuse to call them 'kids' anymore." He picked up a builder set, filled with tiny blocks. "One grandchild, a force of nature. Toby is nine years old, going on twenty."

She led the way up and down the aisle dedicated to technology: spaceships, transformers, action heroes. No sign of any robots. "Let's ask about these mini-GPT3s at the counter."

"I have to tell you, I'm not too hopeful," Matt said. "They're such a hot property, I think if they had any, there would be a big display, lots of posters, that kind of thing."

"You're probably right," Noelle said. "But let's go ask."

The counter was crowded with shoppers trying to get their purchases finished. Three store clerks shared two registers and filled every second with productive activity, and yet they just weren't keeping up. The line stretched past the dollhouses and into the arts and crafts section.

Noelle didn't mind waiting; the scene was quite entertaining. And if there were any possibility that she could buy those robots? She was prepared to wait for as long as it took.

It was almost their turn when earnest voices at the counter drew their attention to a young woman who was trying to buy a life-sized baby doll. It wasn't loud, but it was intense. She seemed to try to convince the store clerk to take her plastic card, but the clerk shook his head, again and again. Suddenly, the young woman burst into tears.

Noelle was uncertain about what to do, but for Matt, there was no hesitation. He stepped forward and said, quietly, "Excuse me, but is there a problem?"

"Her card has been declined," the clerk said. "Three times."

"There's enough money in the account, I know there is!" The woman regained control of herself and held the card out toward the clerk again. "Just try it again."

The man shook his head and reached to take the doll.

As he put it under the counter, the shopper grabbed its leg and held on.

"Hey, careful! You might break it!" The clerk wasn't letting go.

"I have to have that doll! My daughter is counting on it!" The two of them were in a tug-of-war. Matt stepped in again.

"Come on, now," he said in a calming voice. "You could run the card once more, couldn't you? Or perhaps you have another card to try?"

"That's the one that works." The woman hadn't taken her eyes off the doll. "My husband made a payment yesterday and there's enough in there to cover my daughter's gift."

The clerk sighed and took the card, sliding it into the reader. "I'm telling you, man," he said to Matt, "we see this all the time. She wants it, but she doesn't have the money. There!" he said triumphantly, "Told you. Declined. Again."

Noelle unzipped her purse and pulled out her wallet. "And now she has the money. How much is it?"

Matt reached into his back pocket and brought out his wallet, too. "Tag says fifty dollars. With tax? Let's round it up to sixty."

Noelle reached for her cash. "Thirty for me, and thirty for you."

Matt added his thirty and handed the bills to the clerk.

"Oh, no, I couldn't take that." The woman had just returned to normal breathing after her sobbing and almost seemed to be in a state of shock.

"Yes, you can, dear," Noelle said.

Matt smiled as he put his wallet away. "Merry Christmas."

The clerk went back to shaking his head while he stowed the bills in the cash register and put the doll into a bag. He held it out to Matt, who shook his head and motioned to the clerk to give it to the woman who wanted it.

"Thank you so, so much," she said.

Matt smiled at her, with that 'all's right with the world' air that Noelle was beginning to think was one of the most charming things she'd ever seen.

"Merry Christmas," he said again. "And by the way," he said to the clerk, "we're also looking for something for ourselves. Do you have any of the mini GPT3 robots?'

The store clerk snorted. "Not a chance. But I think we're getting some new stock in mid- January."

Matt shook his head. "Too late," he said. "Thanks, anyway."

As they moved away from the counter, making room for the next in the lineup of twenty people waiting for their turn to get a little farther forward on their holiday shopping, Noelle felt as if she'd just come back from a week's vacation on a gorgeous, tropical beach. She realized she was beaming from ear to ear when she caught Matt's eye and realized he was doing the same.

"Donate every time you're asked," Matt said. "Somebody told me that, once. It's not a bad idea."

"But she didn't actually ask you to step in," Noelle said.

"No, but the situation did. The situation called for it. Sometimes that happens and even if I'm not specifically singled out and invited, I know I'm the one being asked. One of the ones, but I don't hide behind the other ones."

Noelle nodded. "I get that."

When they walked out of the store, Matt held out his elbow toward Noelle. "It's a bit icy. May I help?"

She was surprised at how good it felt to take it.

"What's on for you for tomorrow?" Matt asked.

"Sightseeing with the kiddies most-y," Noelle said. "Georgia and Kyle have a big day at work and so I'll pitch in. Tonight, we're having a nice, family Sunday dinner." She wondered for a moment if it was rude of her not to invite him along, but she was looking forward to some relaxing time, getting reacquainted with Georgia. The moment wasn't the least bit awkward, though. It was amazing how easy it was to be with him.

"I wonder if you would let me show you, and Kenneth and Kelsey, around for a while tomorrow afternoon. The New York Botanical Garden has a train that they might like. We can see Times Square, and the waterfront too, if you like."

"I would like, Matt. Thank you."

"Thank you, ma'am," Matt raised his arm to flag down a taxi.

The snow had begun to fall softly. It was just a few flakes, but he reached up a hand to brush them from her hair. Again, that magnetic smile. Noelle knew that in some situations or in a film, she'd find that move cheesy and fake. But it didn't feel that way right now.

CHAPTER 8

When Noelle walked through the lobby after the cab dropped her off, she saw a bubble of activity just to the left of the bank of elevators.

Long tables draped in white linen cloths had been set up and several dozen people clustered around them.

When Noelle got closer, she saw that small plates, cutlery, and glasses anchored one end of each table, with platters of meats, cheeses, and pastries covering every inch that wasn't decked out with holly, red and green glass balls, and tiny, twinkling Christmas elves ornaments.

Servers in white shirts and black pants moved around the tables, helping guests find just the right cookies or tarts and whisking the dirty plates off to the kitchen before anyone noticed them.

Noelle saw Chef Justin circulating among the tables, occasionally summoning one of the servers over to replace a plate of sweet or savory treats that had been picked bare. He raised a hand to wave at her, and she walked over to meet him.

"Chef Justin, this looks amazing."

"It's a dress rehearsal for the Charles Dickens Buffet on Christmas Eve. Chef likes to try out some of his recipes ahead of time. It's a test run, in a way."

"Chef? I thought you were the chef."

"I am chef de cuisine. I run the kitchen. But my boss, Chef Olivier, he is the designer, the mind behind it all. He creates the menus."

"With your help, I'll bet." Noelle reached over to scoop up a particularly appealing slice of lemon loaf.

Justin laughed. "Oh yes, I have my opinions."

"This is delicious," Noelle said as she tasted the cake. "I'll just bet your entire buffet will be, too."

"It's one of the biggest events of the year, for us. We've been getting ready since Labor Day. The theme is Victorian Christmas and chef has a lot of dishes that are authentic to that time," Justin said. "We have quite a few others that are New York specialties, too."

"Would the kiddies enjoy it?"

"Oh yes, lots of goodies for children. In fact, why don't you bring them around on Friday morning? They can see everything being prepared. And take some of these up with you!" he said.

He called to one of the servers. "Simone! Bring me some of those to-go boxes. I could use some honest reviews of the pizza and the mac and cheese."

"We'll be there," Noelle laughed. "But I think I'll line up for something other than mac and cheese, if you don't mind."

She could see his gaze wandering away from her, and

he saw her noticing. "Excuse me, Noelle. I'm kinda expecting Harmonie to drop by. She said she would."

"Are you two an item?" Noelle smiled. "Does anybody say that anymore?"

"I get your meaning," Justin said. "I hope so, soon. Got any advice for me?"

"Don't hesitate," Noelle said, surprising herself. Last week, if anyone had asked her if she had an opinion, she would have said 'no'.

Justin grinned. "That's what I was thinking."

When Noelle got back to the suite, she was not exactly thrilled to find Kyle's mother enthroned in one of the wing-back chairs, watching the kiddies watch television. Pamela had a wine glass in her hand and was wearing an elegant little black dress.

"We have an extra guest for dinner?" Noelle murmured to Georgia as they both stood in front of the floor-to-ceiling windows, admiring the view of the city. "I was hoping for a quiet Sunday dinner. Just us."

"Mom, I think Pamela wants her family time just as much as you do," Georgia said.

Of course. Noelle had to kick herself mentally. She knew she was being selfish. At least, that was what she was supposed to think about her reaction.

The truth was, though, that she could imagine all sorts of reasons that her claim on her grandchildren's time and attention should come first. She was the one who had flown hundreds of miles, on very short notice, to be in a place she didn't like, at the busiest time of the year. She was the one who was being asked to look after them.

"Georgia, it looks like you're getting low on white wine." Pamela stood behind them. "I can arrange to have some sent up."

"Oh, no, Pamela, I'll take care of that," Georgia said as she walked over toward the room phone. "There's a few things I need to get from room service."

"How was your day, Noelle?" Pamela asked, taking up Georgia's spot, facing the view down to Park Avenue. "Very nice, thanks. You?"

Pamela nodded and moved her mouth in what might have been a smile. They both watched the snowflakes fall in silence for a few minutes.

Noelle didn't know what had opened up this big hole between her and Pamela. They had very little in common; that seemed obvious. But they were both women, and they both loved Kelsey and Kenneth. Wouldn't that be enough?

Pamela seemed restless. "Noelle, I probably should keep this to myself, but I just have to say I was really upset by what happened yesterday."

"Really? Because you didn't seem upset."

"Well, I was. I told Georgia it might be a better idea not to have you take them out, right before Christmas."

"You're right, it's a total zoo, here," Noelle said.

Pamela stared at her. "I've lived in New York for twenty years and I've never known anybody who lost a child like that, and had to have the police come. And the TV news! My God, we almost couldn't believe it, when we heard what was going on."

"Almost," Noelle said wryly, looking around for a drink.

"I know you're going to be spending a lot of time with the grandchildren while you're here, especially since Georgia and Kyle have so much work to do this week. Don't you think it would be a better idea if you entertained them here at the hotel? Maybe even, right here—it's a beautiful suite, don't you think?"

Noelle didn't know how to respond to Pamela's question.

Then, she was saved by the Geor-gia bell.

"Mom, can I pour you a glass of wine?" Georgia asked. "I've got them bringing up a selection, and a few more nibbles for the kids."

"Yes, just excuse me, I have to go speak to Kyle," Pamela said as she headed off down the hallway. She certainly seemed to know where everything was.

Noelle took the glass from Georgia.

"What's our dinner plan?" Noelle asked. Better not to be too vague, she was learning. Better to come right out with it. "I thought Sunday evening would be a family dinner at a nice New York restaurant somewhere. I've been in town two days and I've barely seen you."

But Georgia had other things on her mind. "Mom, we still don't have our presentation ready and it's the most important one we'll do all year. If we don't get this client to the maximum shelf space, our summer numbers will be toast. But if we get this right, we could be Featured Toy of the summer!"

Ooh, featured toy of the summer! Well, la di da. Noelle was hurt, but she tried never to let Georgia—or Daisy— know when she disapproved of their choices.

"All right, well . . . maybe tomorrow night."

"Yes, tomorrow night! Daisy will be here by then—"

"Daisy! Daisy is coming?"

"She and Trevor decided to bring Frost to New York to see the sights."

"All the way from Portland? They have lights there, don't they?"

"I think it had something to do with you being here, too," Georgia said.

"Why wouldn't she call and tell me?"

"Because she knew I'd tell you, Mom. Anyway, Kyle and I have to get going. We're due for a meeting in Tribeca in an hour." She called toward the office. "Kyle, come on, we have to leave!"

"But what about Kelsey and Kenneth?" Noelle asked.

"Well," Georgia seemed flustered. "We thought you were in for the evening now. The kids are looking forward to you hanging out with them."

Hanging out? Is that what we call it now?

Kyle walked in, carrying a black overcoat. Pamela stood up, and he held it up for her to put on. "Georgia, we're going to share a cab with Mom," he said.

"You're on your way?" Noelle asked Pamela. "Or maybe you'd like to stay longer, 'hang out' with the kiddies and me."

Pamela nodded in Noelle's direction; it would be too generous to call it a smile. "Thanks, Noelle, but I have plans for this evening."

"Kyle, our meeting is in another part of the city," Georgia said. "But we can get your mother a cab at the front door when we're leaving."

The look from Kyle was like the kind Sherry used to call "the death stare" when it came her way from her husband, Roger. Her third husband. Of five.

"It's not out of our way," Kyle said. "Of course, we'll drop you off, Mom." He pulled on his overcoat. Then there was a flurry of quick hugs with the children, and they were out the door and gone.

Noelle looked around the hotel suite and at the up-turned faces of the two little ones.

"What are we going to do now, Nonny?"

"We'll have our Sunday dinner, just like I planned, but we'll have it here, then find a good movie on TV."

Kenneth looked around the room. "But there's no food here. It's a house with no food and no kitchen."

"We're going to have something called Room Service."

"What's that?"

"We can ask for any food we want and a server will bring it to our room." Noelle sat down on the couch with the menu and a grandchild on each side. "Here, I'll read you the list of what they have."

But when the knock came at the door, signaling the arrival of their dinners, it was not a server who brought it. It was Chef Justin.

Kenneth, who reached the door first in the stampede to answer it, stood in awe in front of a tall figure in white pants, jacket, and hat. "Are you an angel?" he asked.

Justin was startled, but Noelle laughed. "Well, I hear his sauce Béarnaise is heavenly."

"Heard from?" Justin asked. "One of the other guests?"

"One of your co-workers," Noelle said. "One who is very impressed with more than your cooking, I think."

Who didn't like to have a little match-making hobby?

Noelle looked at the silver plate covers on the white linen-covered tray on wheels that he had pushed to the door.

"Is there anything that sophisticated under here?"

Justin pushed the cart into the room, then lifted the plate covers with a flourish. "You'll get to try some of my other sauces at the Dickens Buffet on Christmas Eve. For now, we have spaghetti with meatballs for one, hot dog and fries for another, and a Caesar salad. Plus, three dishes of ice cream."

"Ice cream! Nonny, I didn't know we were having ice cream!" Kelsey ran over and wrapped her arms around Noelle's knees.

"To go with those sugar cookies from the tin we opened this morning," Noelle said. "I'm assuming there are a few left?"

"I'll get them!" Kenneth and Kelsey both ran off toward the buffet table in the dining room.

"It looks delicious," Noelle said, looking over the plates of food. "And thank you so much for bringing it up."

"I do this once or twice a night on the room service orders," Justin said. "It's nice to get out of the kitchen and meet some of my guests."

Kenneth arrived back at the door, a cookie tin under one arm and a little sister-shadow at his side. He was getting pretty low in the fuel tank of good manners. "Can we eat?"

"Yes, in front of the TV."

"In front of the TV? Nonny, you're the best!" Kenneth and Kelsey ran to the couch and sat themselves down.

Expectations were high. Noelle started to prepare their plates, but Justin interrupted her.

"Allow me," he said, as he put a fork and spoon beside the spaghetti, poured some marinara sauce on the fries, then brought them over to the kiddies.

Kenneth's smile was huge. "And cookies for dessert!" He had the bright red tin with the Christmas trees on the lid on the couch cushion beside him. "Nonny brought them with her!"

"You have a very nice grandma," Justin said. "What kind are they?"

"The yummy kind," Kelsey said, holding one out for Justin to nibble.

"Mmm," he said. "Shortbread."

Noelle's phone buzzed with a text. From Dan Keyes.

Hey there. My editor is pushing for this feature about a happy woman showing the magic City of New York to her grandkids at the most wonderful time of the year. Can you help me out, Noelle?

Well, really. He just wasn't going to give up.

In case you've forgotten, or there is more than one TV reporter wanting a tiny slice of your time this week, it's Dan Keyes. Channel 45.

Noelle tried to think of the words to use in her reply text. This was quite a challenge because she hadn't decided yet whether she was going to say 'yes' or 'no'. She actually had already said 'no', but he didn't seem to have heard her.

She still hadn't sorted it out when her phone buzzed again. It was Georgia.

We heard from the TV station again, Mom. Sounds like it will be a terrific souvenir experience to have, the kids on TV in New York. Please, won't you do it?

Justin spotted the frown on her face. "Is something wrong?"

"Oh, no. Just something I need to shake off," Noelle said. "I'm getting a lot of pressure to agree to be in a TV feature about my experiences taking my grandchildren around New York over the holidays."

Chef Justin was one of those who look at a person intently when they speak. "And you don't want to. Pressure from who?"

"From my daughter, their mother. And from the news reporter."

Justin looked at the TV set and, following his glance, Noelle saw Dan Keyes standing in front of the Rockefeller Center tree, chatting with a group of tourists and looking very cute.

"Let's change the channel, shall we?" she said, grabbing for the remote control and punching the "Last" button. The screen immediately switched to a cartoon, and she relaxed.

They heard a knock at the door. "Room service." Justin opened the door. "Room service for Ms. Moran."

The bell hop held a small Christmas tree, fully decorated,

in his right hand.

The little ones were dazzled. "A tree! A little tree!"

"Is it ours?"

"Where can we put it?"

The bell hop carried it in and put it on the coffee table.

"But where did it come from?" Noelle asked. "Is there a note?"

"Sorry, no. No note," the bellhop said.

"Maybe the hotel management?"

Justin and the bellhop exchanged glances. "No, I don't think we do anything like that," Justin said.

"Mommy or Daddy," Kenneth said, as he parked two of his toy cars underneath it.

Noelle looked at him. "Good guess, Kenneth. We'll ask them about it tonight, after they get back from their meetings."

******

It was very late by that time, and the kids weren't able to keep their eyes open long enough to see their parents come in.

Noelle let them fall asleep in front of the TV, then picked them up and carried them off to bed.

When Georgia and Kyle arrived, just a few minutes before midnight, neither one had anything much to say about the Christmas tree delivery and they weren't particularly curious about it.

"Probably from the hotel," Kyle said as he collapsed onto the couch and turned on the TV.

"But why wouldn't Chef Justin know about it?"

Kyle shrugged. "Different department. It's a big hotel."

"You're probably right," Noelle said. "I'm going to bed. Are you going to be around tomorrow?"

"I think so, Mom. What do you have planned? Did you say you'd meet with the TV reporter?"

"I have two appointments tomorrow, actually. Matt and Dan."

Kyle raised an eyebrow, and Noelle responded. "Dan is the TV reporter and Matt is a new friend."

"But why are they both coming by tomorrow, Mom?" Georgia flopped down on the side chair, her legs up over the arm, the way she used to when she was a teenager.

"They're not both 'coming by', dear. They'll be here one at a time. Dan in the morning, Matt in the afternoon."

"Sounds like a musical number," Kyle said. Noelle took a quick look to see whether it was affectionate teasing, but it wasn't. It was meant as sarcasm.

"I understand about the TV reporter. In fact, I'm in favor of it. You know that, Mom. But this other one, this Matt, what's he about?"

It hadn't occurred to you that maybe he just wanted to get to know me? Noelle picked up the TV remote. Maybe she could end this conversation by getting them interested in something on a screen?

Kyle reached over and took the remote from her.

"Be careful," he said.

CHAPTER 9

Matt stood in front of his wall-wide windows, taking in the view of Central Park.

Usually, on a Monday morning, he'd be behind his desk by this time of day, directing the activities of the fifth largest hospital in New York. Even on the last Monday before Christmas—people didn't stop getting sick just because a particular calendar date had rolled around. If anything, there seemed to be more going on at a hospital, not less—lives to save, emergencies to meet, people's health and safety to pro-tect.

But a month ago, he'd sat behind that desk for the final time, gone for a walk through the hallways and the wards to say his goodbyes to the staff and a few special patients, and then let colleagues and friends send him off at a retirement lunch at one of the best restaurants in the city.

Sent him off to where, he didn't know exactly. So far, it felt like nowhere.

**

"Be careful," Kyle had said. But Noelle felt that she didn't want to be careful. That morning, when she went down-stairs to the lobby to keep her appointment with Dan Keyes, it surprised Noelle to feel herself looking forward to seeing the TV newsman again. And definitely, feeling very curious. And adventurous.

The elevator doors opened on a busy scene, with staff zipping back and forth, like trains on a dozen sidetracks in a rail yard. Everything glittered in the reflection of the holiday décor, and each time the front doors opened to let guests in or out, there was a fresh blast of crisp air. Noelle scanned the vast room and saw Dan sitting in an armchair by the fire-place.

"Hi," she said, with a smile as she dropped into the chair beside him.

Now that she wasn't in a stressed-out state and could see him up close, she appreciated again that Dan Keyes was quite a good-looker. Hot, as they'd say nowadays. Hot fifty. His hair was a salt-and-pepper gray, cut in a style that suited his face and matched by a beard trimmed perfectly, around a very square jaw. He wore a suit and tie, the right look for New York City on a Monday morning, but far too formal for the mood Noelle was in.

"Hey yourself," he replied. "Thanks for letting me set this up. How's the little girl?"

"Oh, Kelsey is just fine. It was all just a big adventure to her."

"She's quite a little character." Dan looked around

into the air over her head. "Can I order you a cup of coffee?"

"I don't think the lobby service starts until later. And no, thanks, I've had coffee and breakfast. What's up, Dan?"

"Okay, no small talk. I like that." Dan leaned forward and captured her gaze with his own. "I pitched my assignment editor with a feature about your family and she said yes."

"A feature? What do you mean?"

"Your grandkids are adorable. They're seeing New York at Christmas time and it's magical for them. For you, it's magical to watch their reactions. I'll follow the three of you around the city, you'll see the sights, hit the toy stores. "

Noelle was already shaking her head. "No, I don't think so."

"Why not?" His look was a mixture of surprise and something else. Irritation? Annoyance? He seemed to catch it quickly and shove it down.

She laughed, to take the edge off the rejection. "I'd have to do my hair every day. Worry about the way I look, my clothes—"

"We'll get you a stylist. The camera will be mostly on the kids, anyway."

"So, I wouldn't be on camera?" That changed things somewhat.

"I didn't say that. Just not all the time."

The whole idea made Noelle nervous. But also intrigued, she had to admit to herself. "I doubt that Georgia and Kyle would go for this."

"I think you'd be surprised, Noelle. Is it okay that I call you that? You'd be surprised how much people love to be on TV. And these days, a lot of people have their own little TV shows going on their social media. Heck, they even call them networks!" Dan laughed.

It was nice to see an older man with a cheery expression on his face: so many of them looked as though they were ready to pick a fight at any moment. But, then, so did a lot of women.

"I don't know, Mr. Keyes. I don't think it's my call. It's up to their parents."

"Yes, of course. But please. Call me Dan. Look, there's no payment involved in something like this, but maybe I could arrange for something that would make it worth your while. A helicopter tour of the city? Is there anybody you or your grandkids would like to meet? Basketball player? Hockey player?"

Noelle shook her head. "You're really on the wrong track if you think I'm looking for some sort of compensation. I used to be a schoolteacher. You don't go into that line of work if getting rich is your goal."

"Please. Don't get huffy. I just know that something like this takes up your valuable time. And it's the week before Christmas. You're devoting yourself to your grandkids. Why would you want to help me do my job?" He smiled again and she knew she wouldn't mind helping a man like this do his job.

Noelle returned the smile. "Alright, I won't get huffy. What a strange word."

Dan laughed. "It really is. Anyway, what should we do, to explore this? Should I give the children's mother another call?"

"I'll talk to her," Noelle said. "But I still need to spend

a little time, deciding what I think about your request."

Dan looked off across the lobby, distracted by a large family group that had arrived with what appeared to be four pieces of luggage each.

"Yes, of course," he said, "and in the meantime, I'll try to think of what else I could say that might convince you. It will be fun, I promise. I can help you cut the line anywhere you want to get in. Let's see . . . you don't like money . . . Maybe I can help you find a pair of those robot toys all the kids are so crazy about this year?"

That got Noelle's attention. Could he really do that? "Is that what you do? Keep on coming at people, trying various levers, until you find the right one?"

Dan laughed. "Pretty much. When the straight-up bribes don't work."

"I'll think about it and get back to you," she said.

Dan took her cue and stood up. "That's great. I'll call you later today. Maybe around noon? We could get started after lunch and have something ready for tonight's cast."

"Whoa, Mr. Keyes. I haven't said we'd do it."

"Dan. Please. 'Mr. Keyes' makes me feel like a stranger." Dan looked around the lobby in a way that suggested she was supposed to be following along, noting the places his attention focused: the Christmas trees, the decorations over the reception desk, the lights sur-rounding the front doors. "God, I love Christmas, don't you? I know a lot of people get cynical about it, but I still think it's the best time of the year. I remember every year right back to when I was a kid. I think those were the best times, really. My mother used to make these amazing fruitcakes from a recipe that her mother gave her. Christmas dinner was a really big deal, with turkey and all the trimmings. Christmas breakfast was a big deal, too. And Christmas Eve! My brothers came home from wherever they were, everybody came home. And my mother was the center of it all. Yeah, the best time of the year."

Dan patted her on the shoulder. "Thanks for your time this morning. I'll be looking forward to your phone call and your answer, Noelle."

**

When Noelle got back to the suite, she walked in on a scene of chaos. Georgia was chasing Kelsey around the dining room table, trying to get her to sit down and finish her breakfast. Kenneth was cheering Kelsey on. Kyle was nowhere to be seen.

"Mom! Awesome, you're back. Could you please get Kelsey to eat her breakfast? I'm going to be late for my presentation if I don't leave in the next five minutes."

Georgia was still wearing one of the hotel bathrobes. "I'd say you'd better get moving." Noelle reached for the breakfast plate.

"It's a huge opportunity, this meeting," Georgia said as she disappeared into the bedroom.

Fifteen minutes later, after Noelle had charmed both Kelsey and Kenneth into eating their fruit, cereal, yoghurt, milk, and chewy vitamins, Kyle and Georgia emerged, her tailored suit, crisp white blouse, and elegant pumps a perfect match for his New York City executive look.

As a pair, they reminded Noelle of something from a

banking commercial, even though their industry was toys. But it was all about making money, she supposed, and serious work required serious clothes.

"Well, look at you two. If I were in charge, I'd decide to promote you."

"There's nowhere to promote to, Mom," Georgia said. "We are both exec VPs, and we own part of the company."

Almost everything I say seems to get under Georgia's skin these days, Noelle thought.

"Not really the kind of decision you've ever made in your life as a schoolteacher," Kyle said. "Former schoolteacher, I should say."

Apparently, her son-in-law's skin was quite thin, too.

Noelle took Georgia's elbow to draw her over toward the door and away from the table where the little ones were sitting.

In a low voice, she said, "I'm still looking for the mini-GPT3 robots for Kenneth and Kelsey. And for Frost. I don't suppose with your toy company connections you might hear on the grapevine where there might be some supply?"

Kyle followed them. "My mother is hunting for those, too, Noelle," he said. "She has standing orders in at every toy store in town and there just aren't any."

He held up Georgia's coat for her. "But if anybody is going to come up with one, it's her. There's no point in you trying to order one now, Noelle. It's too late."

"Well, I entered a contest," Noelle said. "I might get one there."

Kyle shook his head with a look of pity. Then, in a

whoosh of hurry and energy that reminded her of the action thirty-five floors below on the streets and sidewalks, Georgia and Kyle departed.

Noelle took the opportunity to bring the kiddies onto the couch beside her for a cuddle and a book. Amazing how calm and serene the room seemed, now that she was alone with the little ones.

"Nonny, where did our Christmas tree come from again?" Kenneth asked. "Was it the man in the white jacket?"

"The angel," Kelsey said, nestling against Noelle's side.

"No, that was Chef Justin," Noelle said. "He brought you your dinners. Somebody else sent the tree."

Who did send the tree?

There was a knock at the door and a low voice. "Room service."

"What are we getting, Nonny?" The kids were already racing toward the door.

"I didn't order anything, sweetie. You wait here and I'll answer it."

An older man in a hotel uniform handed over an envelope, smiled at her, and headed off toward the elevator.

It was hotel stationery. Noelle opened it and read the note aloud. "The tree from last night was so that you'll have a tree in your room. That little guy has a partner somewhere in NYC and this afternoon we'll have a treasure hunt to find it. See you and your grandkids about eleven? Matt."

Matt. She should have guessed. Noelle tucked the note into her purse, then checked the clock. Just enough time to get ready. A quick text to Matt, a game of "I Spy" while she enticed the kiddies into their clothes, coats, and boots, an elevator ride, and then they were ready and waiting in the lobby.

Five days until Christmas. Noelle could feel the energy in the hotel ramping up, almost by the minute. A crowd of high school kids was bunched around the reception desk, waiting to check in. The lineup to the concierge desk wound around one of the giant Christmas trees and out into one of the hallways. Donald, the concierge, looked even more harassed and unpleasant than usual.

Kenneth was so excited he could barely breathe.

Noelle felt a bit overwhelmed by the sheer size of the human tide running through the lobby, and when she saw Matt walk in through the revolving door, she almost cheered.

"There's my friend, Matt," she told Kenneth. "He is going to take us out for an adventure."

Matt squatted down to get to the little boy's level. Kenneth looked him in the eye, then let loose with a barrage of questions. "Where are we going? How will we get there? Is Kelsey going, too? Can I bring my cars?"

"We're going for a ride in my car and then a ride on a boat," Matt said. "It's called the Staten Island Ferry. Then we're going to Brooklyn and we'll see some Christmas trees. Yes, Kelsey and your grandma are going, too. I don't want you to lose any of your cars and you might be too busy to keep a close watch on them."

"Just this one?" He held up his right hand. Matt grinned. "All right, one."

Kenneth stretched out his left hand and opened his fingers. "And you be in charge of this one."

Matt caught the toy car that fell from Kenneth's palm. "You bet, I'm in charge."

"Are we getting our big tree now?" Kenneth asked.

"On the way back from the boat," Matt said. "You'll see. There are trees for sale on almost every corner, and if we can't find one here, we'll go to Brooklyn. Come on, we're going in this big car just outside," he said to Noelle and Kelsey, holding the door for them. "There's a special seat for you and one for your sister," he told Kenneth.

Noelle tucked herself into the passenger seat beside Matt. Kenneth objected to the car seat, describing it as "for babies" until Matt pointed out that they'd be able to see a lot more, perched up high like that.

"Try it," he said, and the little boy agreed.

"One more thing," Matt said, his eyes on the traffic as he pulled away from the hotel entrance. "What should I call you? Do you like Kenneth or—"

"Kenny. Call me Kenny." No uncertainty there.

"Alright, Kenny. Buckle up and hang on! We're heading for the Staten Island Ferry!"

Noelle kept them busy looking for red or green cars all the way. The snow had let up and the sidewalks were crowded with shoppers hunting for special gifts on these last few days before Christmas.

She was grateful that Matt hadn't asked if she wanted a stop to tour the Statue of Liberty as well. She'd love to see it herself, but when she'd asked the little ones about it, earlier in her visit, they hadn't understood a word of what she was saying.

So—she'd see it another time. After all, she'd get back

to New York again, wouldn't she? And if not, oh well. The comfort of the children was more important than anything else.

She realized that Matt had chosen a route that would take them past Radio City Music Hall when she saw the lights of the Rockefeller Center tree just up ahead.

"There's a good tree!" Kenneth said. "Can we get that one to take back to the hotel for our Christmas?"

"It's a bit too big," Matt said. "And it's there so that everybody can see it and enjoy it. The one we're going to get will be just for your family."

"You know, I came by here the other day on the way in from the airport and there was a cat up the tree," Noelle said.

"A cat!" All three spoke simultane-ously, Kenneth and Kelsey intrigued with the idea and Matt amused.

"I doubt very much there was a cat up that tree," Matt said.

Noelle heard the teasing in his voice. "There was! The fire department was here and everything! You ask the cab driver, he'll tell you."

Matt laughed. "Yes, we'll find him and get him to back up your story. Got his name and number, did you?" He made a left at the intersection and they pulled into a street even more crowded than the previous one. "Besides, the fire department doesn't come to bring cats down from trees these days. I think you're still operating on your old New York impressions."

"You might be right. But it was a pretty impressive impression," Noelle said. "If they aren't rescuing cats, they should be."

The Ferry would be enough of an adventure. Kenneth was thrilled to be going out on the water; Noelle was thrilled to see how Matt gripped his hand frequently and generally kept an eye on him. She was holding onto Kelsey's hand and wouldn't let go of it, except in the car, all afternoon.

They filed down the stairs toward the bright orange vessel and got seats on a bench, with a great view of the harbor. Noelle had heard of the Staten Island Ferry many times, often from friends who'd return from touring New York and couldn't stop marveling over finding something to do that was free, after coming face to face with thirty-dollar-hamburgers and twenty-dollar salads.

"How long is the trip?" she asked Matt.

"Twenty-five minutes. Five miles," he said. "We can see the Statue of Liberty and Ellis Island from this side."

It was cold and they could see the steam of their breath. Noelle was kept busy helping the kiddies mop their runny noses with tissues from the stash she'd been carrying and replenishing since she'd arrived on Saturday.

After touring the boat on this level from stem to stern six times, they were finally tired enough to drop onto a bench. Noelle handed each of them a new picture book and within minutes they were absorbed in turning pages, their eyes drinking in the images of Santa, elves, and Christmas trees.

"Would you like me to read to you?" she asked.

"No, thank you Nonny, we're just looking," Kenneth said.

Noelle looked out through the windows. "Do you think the view might be better outside?" she said to Matt.

"We could go up to the upper deck on the Jersey side.

It might be colder, but I don't think it would be too crowded . . . and since we're not here at rush hour, there aren't a lot of commuters around."

"Let's do that. I think the kids would enjoy it," Noelle said.

"What about you?" Matt asked. "Would you enjoy it?"

Noelle smiled. "Come on, Kenneth, Kelsey. Let's go upstairs. Hold hands, though, please."

The view from the upper deck was breathtaking. The skyscrapers and bridges almost seemed to sparkle in the bright midday sun. Being out on the water was always exhilarating for Noelle. She turned to wait for Matt and Kenneth.

"It's beautiful up here."

"Yes, it is," Matt said. "Here, let me take Kelsey's hand. You look around a bit."

She felt her heart lift and her face smile, involuntarily; her pace sped up as she headed toward the rail.

The deck was slick, and she should have expected that. Noelle felt her right foot slide and then go into a skid. That's it. I'm going down.

But two seconds later, there was a strong arm around her back and she had her balance again.

"Are you okay?" Matt asked.

"I am," she said. "Thank you. I didn't realize it was so slippery."

For just a moment, everything suddenly stopped. Noelle looked into his eyes and really saw him, all at once. His arm was still around her waist and she felt herself lean into him.

It had been a long time since that had happened, and

if anybody had asked her before this moment, she would have said that it was unlikely ever to happen again: leaning on a man, letting him hold her up, knowing there was something much more than friendship between them.

But it was happening now.

Noelle gave herself a shake. Where were the kiddies? "Where are Kenneth and Kelsey, are they okay? Oh, there they are! Kids, watch your step, it's very slippery."

They both looked at their grandmother as if she had no idea what she was talking about. Noelle let them have a little space but watched them like a mama bear watches cubs.

Matt grinned at her. "You're a wonderful grandma."

"I hear a 'but'."

"No, no 'buts'. They're very lucky to have you and I wonder if they know it."

The Statue was moving into view and Noelle felt a mixture of awe and pride as she stared at it. "Whenever I think of it, or look at a picture of it . . . or at the real thing, like now! I always think of Paris and how it was a gift from France."

"Have you been to Paris?" Matt asked.

"No, but I'd love to see it someday."

She turned to him and saw him studying her face. "I'd take you to Paris," he said softly.

"Nonny!" Both Kenneth and Kelsey were on a mission. "We're hungry!"

"Well, that's a good thing because they have a food concession here that's too full and I heard they really need somebody to come along and take some of these hot dogs off their hands. Two somebodies!"

"Three somebodies! Four some-bodies!" Kelsey giggled.

Once lunch was done, they got off the boat on the Island and got right back on for the return trip. "Christmas tree next?"

Noelle's phone buzzed and she saw Georgia's name. "Just a sec, Matt."

Kyle and I have to work late to-night. Last night I did mention it would be about 12 hrs today.

That's fine, Noelle texted back. The kids and I will be fine.

Thx. btw, that TV guy called again. He still wants to do a story about the kids. Have you thought any more about it?

Noelle put her phone back into her purse. Plenty of time to deal with that later.

"Where to next?" she asked Matt as they climbed into his car.

"I thought we'd make a stop at the Botanical Garden, to see the lights and the train, then go get a tree. If we find a place that delivers, we'll do that. If not, we'll strap it on top and take it over to the hotel when I drop you off," he said.

Noelle was happy to see the kiddies doze off in the car on the way to the Bronx. Nothing worse than over-tired youngsters being expected to behave properly in a public place. When they pulled into the parking lot, she could see lights twinkling and a dome silhouetted against a sky that was beginning to darken.

"Here we are," Matt said. "One of New York's many

hidden gems."

"I've never heard of this," Noelle said.

"Well, it's been here more than a hundred and thirty years," he said, grinning. "I guess you didn't get the memo."

She leaned back against the passenger side door and looked him over. "You know, I know almost nothing about you."

"What do you want to know?"

"Do you have a job?"

Matt laughed. "I used to. I don't need one now. I retired a month ago from running St. Mary's Neurosciences Center."

"It's a bit early to ask you how you like retired life, then," Noelle said. "What else do you do?"

"What do I do?" Matt repeated.

"What are your hobbies, what do you like, what do you hate?"

Matt stared into her eyes. "You know, I don't really know? I haven't had time for hobbies. I liked work, I guess."

"I know the feeling," Noelle said. "You put in all those years and you forget who you are."

"Or you find out you've gradually evaporated," he said, turning to stare out of his car window. "Well. We've certainly become very gloomy all of a sudden. I do know that I like Christmas, and beautifully done gardens, and New York."

"I might go for the middle one there," Noelle said.

"Where's the tree?" a six-year-old voice demanded sleepily.

It took only minutes for Kenneth and Kelsey to be ready for the next part of the adventure. The Garden was home to about a million plants and botanical marvels, but Kenneth and Kelsey had eyes only for the Holiday Train Show.

Noelle had to agree, as she looked at a model of the Statue of Liberty made of acorns and pinecones, that it was spectacular.

Most of the major landmarks were represented: Radio City Music Hall, the Brooklyn Bridge, the Chrysler Building, Yankee Stadium, St. Patrick's Cathedral, and an Empire State Building made of pinecones, palm fronds, and birch bark.

"There must be a hundred of them," she whispered to Matt. Something about the miniature scale of the Holiday Train and the lighting made whispering seem appropriate.

He smiled back at her. "There's something about seeing those monumental architectural things brought down to such a human scale that's just very enjoyable, at this time of year," he said.

While the New York City landmarks mesmerized the adults, for Kenneth, it was all about the train. He stared at the brightly painted engine and cars speeding around the track, then announced, "I want Santa to bring me a train set."

"But you've already told him you want a mini GPT3 robot," Noelle said.

"We have to write him another letter." Kenneth took Noelle's hand. "He'll get it. Come on, Nonny, we have to go back to the hotel so I can write him another letter."

Matt had one more stop planned on his 'get to know and love New York' tour. He explained to Kenneth that Dyker Heights was on the way back to the hotel and that he'd have plenty of time afterward to write a letter to Santa.

They decorated the houses in this Brooklyn neighborhood with lighting displays like nothing Noelle had ever seen before. Giant candy canes, angels, stars, reindeer, and sleighs covered the front yards. Strings of lights traced every line of the eaves and windows. She lost count of the snowmen, polar bears, and angels. You'd bet good money this could be seen from outer space.

On the ride back from Dyker Heights, there was no sound but Christmas music playing softly.

"Just one more thing," Matt said, then pulled the car into a parking spot that magically appeared right beside a Christmas tree lot.

Noelle would have thought the kiddies were exhausted by that point but they perked up and followed Matt enthusiastically up and down the rows of fir and pine trees. The three of them agreed that all the trees were perfect, and did an 'eeny-meeny-miney-moe' to choose the one that Matt attached to his car's roof with bungee cords.

Within minutes of pulling away from the curb, Kenneth and Kelsey fell asleep, their little heads rolling back and forth against the headrests of their car seats. When the car pulled up to the hotel entrance and Matt unsnapped their seat belts, they woke up. After helping them down from the car, Noelle pulled one close to each side of her in a half-hug, and they turned toward the revolving door.

"Thanks so much," she said to Matt. "It's been a wonderful day."

Matt folded a bill into the hand of the doorman, who didn't bat an eye as he called two valets over to help him take the tree down from the roof of the car.

"You can get this up to Ms. Moran's suite, can't you?"

"Yes, of course, sir," the doorman said. "And are we parking the car for you?"

"No, I'm on my way," Matt said. "Thank you for a wonderful day, Noelle."

When the kids were done with their baths, they cuddled up on the couch while Noelle found sheets of hotel stationery for their revised letters to Santa. She also brought out the third tin of cookies, this one a dark blue with shiny silver snowflakes sprinkled over the lid.

"I call these volcano cookies," she said as she held out the tin toward the two excited kids. "Bite into it and it will be all gooey inside."

Kenneth already had his into his mouth. "Mmm."

His little shadow was right behind him. "Mmm."

"Is it gooey because it's like lava?" Kenneth asked.

Noelle was surprised. "You know about lava?"

"We saw it on TV. It comes out of the volcano. But it's hot and you can't step in it. And you don't eat it."

"Exactly," Noelle agreed. "But this is a volcano cookie, not a real volcano. And the lava is warm chocolate, not lava."

Hours after she had tucked them into bed, Noelle sat on the couch, turned so that she could see the night beyond the window. Snow was falling . . . again! The lights in the buildings across the way gave the street a warm, welcoming look.

She flipped on the TV and surfed around, sound off, looking at a few minutes of half a dozen Christmas movies and holiday specials. She had to admit, New York City wasn't nearly that bad, once you got to know it a bit.

She stopped at the news channel when she saw Dan Keyes standing in front of the Dyker Heights lights display they'd seen earlier. The camera came in for a close-up and it looked as though he was speaking through the lens, directly to her. She smiled for a moment and almost turned on the sound.

The hotel suite door opened and Georgia and Kyle wandered in. Both of them looked exhausted. Whatever else she must think about them, they worked hard. Noelle turned off the TV.

"Hey there, you guys," she said. "How was your day?"

Georgia rambled on about spreadsheets and inventory, and Noelle found it hard to keep her mind on what was being said. She was very grateful when Georgia followed Kyle off to the bedroom after about five minutes, leaving her in possession of the living room once again.

Noelle poured herself a brandy from one of the crystal decanters on the sideboard. A late-night drink alone was something she almost never did, ever since Yvonne had warned her of the dangers of letting that become a habit.

But tonight, everything felt different somehow. It felt like a night for a celebration.

The reason she couldn't keep her mind on anything Georgia was saying was Matt. Ever since the moment he'd walked her from his car to the hotel elevator, she'd been replaying the events of the day in her mind. But each time she recalled one place or one moment, thoughts of his eyes, his smile, and his hands distracted her. She hadn't thought she'd spent that much time looking at him, but now she found she remembered many things in great detail. Standing beside him and being so conscious of how he towered over her. His broad shoulders and long legs. His silver hair and blue eyes. But again, most of all, his smile.

Noelle noticed men's smiles, and had seen quite a few in her time. Yvonne said you could tell how a person felt about the way his life turned out by the way he smiled. Some people believed that eyes were the window to the soul, but Noelle believed it was the smile. You could tell by the feeling you had in reaction. Some people just made you feel warm, or even hot. Some left you cold.

Matt's gave her a flutter, somewhere under her ribcage. Really? Oh, come on. She was a woman old enough to be past all that. Besides, she didn't really believe in that 'you really do feel it' stuff. She knew about feelings of attraction, but a feeling of love? An actual, physical feeling?

In Noelle's experience, love was an idea, a thought, a decision, and then an activity and an action. If you love somebody, it means you do things for them, with them, to them. But that was because you'd thought about it and decided. Not because of a physical feeling.

Now, somewhere in Noelle's depths, somewhere inside, something shifted. She'd seen so many smiles that she pretty much thought she'd seen everything. Until she saw his. Everything had changed.

Was she going nuts? Was that what had changed? Noelle stared at her reflection in the window, but nothing there looked any different. Nothing showed the way that she was feeling—and that was a very good thing. She needed to keep this to herself.

Volcano, indeed.

DEVIN AUDRAH

CHAPTER 10

The morning of December 21st dawned cloudy and cold. Noelle had been awake since three, just another one of her 'early rising' days. She wouldn't call it a sleepless night, and she wouldn't call it insomnia, but she often woke up long before sunrise, feeling refreshed and rested on only four or five hours of sleep.

She'd decided years ago not to fight it. Just get up and get on with the day.

When she wandered into the living room of the suite, she found Georgia curled up on the couch with a mug of coffee and her computer.

"How long have you been up?" she asked.

"A while," Georgia said. "Did you have a good day yesterday?"

"Lovely. You?"

Georgia made a face. "Exhausting. Meetings non-stop, then business dinner, then more meetings. Same again today. You're okay with this, aren't you, Mom? You have some plans with the kids?"

One part of Noelle wanted to tell Georgia to get a grip and look at what it was she was really doing. She was going to miss the best years of Kenneth's and Kelsey's childhoods, if she wasn't careful. It wasn't that she expected Georgia (or Kyle) to stop working or quit their jobs, but surely, they could find a few free afternoons the week before Christmas?

"And if I didn't?" Noelle asked.

"The hotel has a really good babysitter program; there's information on it in the room guide. It's over there on the desk."

Georgia looked so concerned that Noelle didn't have the heart to keep her on the hook any longer. A babysitter? When Grandma was right there? At Christmas?

"No, of course not, dear. I'd be happy to look after them again today."

"It might be a late night again."

"Don't worry. I'll be here."

Noelle would not have thought it possible, but Georgia and the kiddies had dislodged Matt from her thoughts. Would he want to spend another full day with them? And her?

He had seemed to enjoy himself around the kids yesterday, but after the discussion about Paris, she'd noticed him staring at her several times, almost transfixed. Kenneth, in particular, had tried to get Matt's attention, and he did respond to the little guy, but most of the afternoon, Matt seemed to have eyes only for Noelle.

She was flattered, but mostly she felt mixed up about it all. Kenneth and Kelsey needed her so much. She'd had her time for romance and love, but that was long ago. It was her time now to be a grandma.

At the tree lot, he'd been happy to go along with the little ones' request that he "take a pitcher', but after getting a few of Kenneth and Kelsey, he'd motioned to Noelle to stand over by herself by a beautiful Douglas fir and he pointed the camera in her direction. She understood—she would have liked to have one of him, too.

Maybe today, they'd get a selfie of the two of them.

The minute she had the thought, she was shocked at herself. She was thinking like a teenager.

"Sorry, what?" Noelle realized that Georgia had asked her a question.

"I said, I heard from that TV reporter again this morning."

"Dan Keyes?"

"That's the one. He's still asking that we give permission for a feature on the kids experiencing a New York Christmas."

"He didn't!"

"He did."

"But I haven't decided whether I even want to do it," Noelle said. "And I have to tell you, I'm leaning toward no."

"No? But why? And why would that be up to you?" Georgia stood up and paced around the living room. "I think the kids would enjoy it and you'd probably get to go into all sorts of places that are really hard to get into. Cut the lines. You know."

"Don't you think it's a better idea to keep their private lives private?"

Georgia looked at her as if she'd suddenly grown a second head. "Everywhere is public, Mom. You take them to the park, that's a public place. And they're so adorable, why wouldn't anybody want to see them?"

"Well, I'm not that adorable, and I don't want to be on TV," Noelle declared. "And I will not spend my day with a news reporter and camera people following me everywhere."

"But—"

"Are you going to take the day off work to be with the kids and put them on TV?" Noelle waited. "I didn't think so." She picked up Georgia's mug. "Do you want some more coffee?"

Georgia took a look at her watch. "No, I have to get ready to go. Incidentally, where did that tree come from?"

"We bought it yesterday while we were out sightseeing."

"Is it going to stay plain like that?"

"I'll pick up some decorations while I'm out today," Noelle said. "You could bring back a few things, too. Hold on a minute, Georgia, I just remembered a text I have to send." She looked down at her phone and began tapping in the letters.

"Won't have time," Kyle said, as he walked in on the conversation. He was completely dressed for the workday. "Come on, Georgia, we have to get going."

Half an hour later, Noelle had waved the two of them off and was standing in the lobby with the kiddies, barely able to hold down her excitement as they waited for Matt to arrive. His reply text had come within seconds of her message, asking if he had another day to spare to be her New York tour Guide.

Kelsey and Kenneth sat on a couch beside the tree, looking at a book. Noelle examined a poster for the Radio City Music Hall Spectacular, but kept one eye on the door, watching for him.

"Good morning!"

Harmonie Randolph looked awfully perky for someone who had probably been working, singing in the lounge, past midnight.

"Hey, how are you?" Noelle asked. "What are you doing up and around so early?"

"We all double up on duties around the holidays," Harmonie said. "If we want to make a little extra money. You're right, it is early for me. I was in the lounge, doing my show, till late last night. But this morning, I'm helping out in the kitchen, making cookies and a few other things for the big buffet we do on Christmas Eve. Are you planning to come? It's incredible, pastries like you've never seen before in your life."

"I thought I heard you objecting to working two jobs the other day."

Harmonie grinned. "That was setting up a banquet room. This is the kitchen."

Noelle grinned back. "With that charming Chef Justin. I get it."

"Do you blame me?" Harmonie asked, just as Justin appeared in the lobby, walking toward them. "I have to go!"

Noelle related to the feeling, but when Matt arrived, she had her game face on. Nobody, least of all Matt, was going to know what she was feeling, not yet.

It was still so new. . . and confusing. What was a woman

her age thinking, letting ideas like those of a teenager in puppy love, go free range through her brain? She was supposed to be mature, for heaven's sake. She had no time for something like this. Her daughter needed her and her grandchildren needed her more.

The day was going to be a dazzler. Matt had obviously spent some time planning. The first part of the morning included an itinerary on wheels—past the Empire State Building, Times Square, Fifth Avenue, Herald Square, Greenwich Village, Seventh Avenue, and past Madison Square Garden, its giant marquee advertising a New Year's Eve concert and a hockey game the next week.

Noelle had seen yesterday that Matt was very skilled at stick-handling through the traffic and today, four days before Christmas, even as they got closer to the tourist gridlock, he found many openings to slide through.

Times Square was like a Christmas light display, amplified a million times. Noelle almost felt that she needed sunglasses against the glare.

Just when she thought they were going to see it only through the car window, Matt pulled the steering wheel to the right and into a parking lot that she never would have guessed was there.

"Come on!" he said, as he unbuckled the car seats and helped the kids down from the car. "There's a place here where we can go to get tickets. Tickets! Do we all love tickets? Yes, we do!"

Leading a pair of excited, applauding youngsters (who had no idea what tickets were but knew they wanted to have some) and their intrigued grandma through the crowds, Matt guided them to the ticket office in Times Square.

The lines were long, but the signs announced that there were still plenty of seats to be had for Broadway shows. Good seats and great seats.

"What are we doing?" she whispered to Matt. If this was to be his secret, and a surprise for the kiddies, she didn't want to be the one to blow it open. Noelle loved a surprise herself.

"You'll see," he whispered back.

He reached over to squeeze her hand, and even through the gloves she wore, she felt the heat. She looked into his laughing eyes and somehow the moment caught and time froze. Thousands of passersby blurred and faded into the background.

Time stopped.

She'd seen this depicted in movies dozens of times, and often thought it was totally cheesy. Didn't happen in real life—at least, never to her. Maybe that had been the problem?

She became aware that Kenneth was staring at them, his gaze like a furnace blast. His little eyes blazed at her and his forehead furrowed. Was that a six-year-old's unspoken message of possessiveness?

Kenneth stepped forward and grabbed his grandma's hand, tugging her in the direction of the ticket booth. She knew he had no idea where he was going, just that he wanted to go. She rolled her eyes in Matt's direction, but allowed herself to be pulled.

Matt reached for Kelsey's hand. "I heard you saying that you wanted to see the Nutcracker Ballet and this is where we can pick up last-minute tickets."

Noelle was delighted. But her experience with men had her questioning the wisdom of putting Matt in a lineup for tickets. Wasn't it the sort of thing that made all men irritable? "Are you sure that's what you want to be doing?"

"We'll try to get six," he said. "Then we have enough, if Kyle and Georgia want to come along. What evening or matinée should we try for?"

"They have their company holiday party on Thursday night, so that leaves tomorrow," Noelle said.

"Let's see what we can do."

It wasn't freezing and Noelle was grateful that the snow had stopped falling for a while. The people in the line were all in a good mood and the time passed quickly. Huge video screens carrying features about New York holiday activities and news added to the festive feeling.

As Noelle watched, one of the screens displayed a Channel 45 piece about this year's parade. Dan Keyes appeared, doing commentary from the sidelines.

"Hey, there's that reporter who showed up at Santa's workshop," Noelle said. "Do you remember him?"

Matt didn't look up. "Yeah, I remember him. He seems to turn up all over the place."

When they were two groups short of the front of the line, Noelle got a text from Daisy. Now there was a name she hadn't seen on her incoming call display that often lately.

Surprise! We're in New York now too. What are you doing?

Matt noticed. Was he going to notice every expression on her face from now on? She'd never felt so seen.

She met his eyes and his unspoken question. "It's my daughter."

"They're taking a break from the toy maker meetings?"

"Ha. No, my other daughter."

"Other daughter?"

"Daisy is two years younger. Lives in Portland, Maine." Noelle pulled her gloves off to text.

Getting tickets.

Daisy was back in a second.

Yay. Get some for us too. What are they for?

Noelle sighed, then gave her full attention to Matt. "She lives in Portland, but she's here in New York, apparently. She and her husband and son came into town for the holidays, to see everybody. We'll get together with them soon but in the meantime, she's asking to be added to the group for whatever it is we're planning to see."

Matt laughed. "You look like someone just stole your dog. Or your car or your favorite shoes or something. The more the merrier, right? We'll just get three more."

Okay, nine tickets. What would they do if there weren't enough for everybody? Who would they leave out?

But when they got to the ticket window, there were none left for the Nutcracker at all. From delighted to disappointed, in a nano-second. Noelle covered it up, though. That's what she did. They walked a few feet away, trying to decide what to do next.

"I'll be back in a minute," Matt said.

He walked back to the window they'd just left, said something and then unleashed his mega-watt smile on the person standing at the wicket, pulled out his wallet and handed over a card.

When he came back, he looked like the quarterback who's just thrown the winning pass.

"This is almost as good," he said. "Better, some New Yorkers might tell you. Especially those without the taste for classical music."

"What are they, Matt?"

"Radio City Christmas Spectacular," he said, holding four tickets toward her.

Noelle took them. "I don't know . . . is it good? I know what the Nutcracker Ballet is but I've never heard of this one."

"That's because you don't come to New York enough," Matt said with a serious tone. "It's famous here, and it's the best. The kids will love it."

She was still doubtful, and not too sure how she felt about his impulsiveness in buying the tickets without run-ning the idea past her.

She also felt as though she ought to offer to pay for their three tickets, or at least half of it all. This was New York; who knew how many hundreds of dollars that might be?

"The best, huh?" she said. "We're still working the 'New York is better than anywhere else' thing? How do you know I haven't seen a holiday play in Vermont that outshines anything you have here?"

"I'm sure you have, Noelle," he grinned back at her.

"I take it back. It's not the best, and New York is not everybody's cup of coffee. I will stop raving about it and pushing you to like it as much as I do."

"No, you won't."

Man, those eyes of his were something.

"Give it a chance, Noelle. Come on."

"What's going on, Nonny? Why are we standing here?" Kenneth had been watching the back and forth between Matt and Noelle, and something was bothering him.

"Mr. Matt has bought us tickets to see a show all about Christmas," Noelle said.

"What, all about Christmas?" Kelsey wanted to know more."

"It's at Radio City Music Hall, the most famous theater in New York. We're going to see elves, and Santa, and toy soldiers, and dancers, and reindeer. Real ones!"

Even Noelle wasn't sure she believed him on that last one. The kiddies looked like he was telling the biggest whopper they'd ever heard.

"Come on, we have to get a move on," Matt said. "It starts in two hours and we haven't had lunch yet."

"Two hours! But Georgia and Kyle won't be able to get over here that fast!" Noelle said.

Matt smiled. "That works out then, because there were only four seats left."

**

Noelle texted Daisy from the car on the way to the restaurant.

Hey, hi! Welcome to New York! Delighted you guys are here— can't wait to see you!

Daisy was right back, instantly.

Me, too! Where are you, right now?

In Manhattan.

Long pause, probably while Daisy took this in and thought over her answer. Was her mother being deliberately vague? Or did she really think a literal, detailed answer like that was what was called for?

Or maybe Daisy wasn't thinking about her mother's text at all. Maybe, she just had to use the bathroom and had only just returned to her phone. Noelle knew sometimes she gave far too much analysis to her texts and other communications with her daughters. This was one of them.

She wrapped it up quickly.

Looking forward to seeing you later. Bye.

"Everything okay?" Matt glanced over from his spot behind the wheel.

"Yes, everything's good." Noelle's phone buzzed again. Georgia, this time.

Did you get the ballet tickets?

You know, we couldn't get those. Sold out. But we did get some to see the Radio City Christmas Spectacular.

I've heard that's a really good one!

We're going as Matt's guests.

I read it's sold-out months in advance.

Matt got last-minute tickets. But only 4. And it's on in two hours.

Two hours! I'm in a meeting

Not expecting you or Kyle

After five minutes with no response, Noelle felt the need to add to her message.

I'm sorry Matt couldn't get enough tickets for you too but you said you were busy all day.

Another long pause.

Who IS this guy?

Noelle had to stop the text volley for a minute to consider that one. Who was this guy?

Matt likes the theater. She doubted that would shed much light for Georgia but it was all she had, at the moment.

Gotta go, lunch is ready. We'll be back at the hotel by 5.

Lunch wasn't really ready, but this text string with Georgia was really killing her buzz. She wasn't sure why—was it possible that she felt guilty? About what? Not getting enough tickets for everybody? Turning down a request from her daughter? Spending a few hours with a new friend?

Matt's plan for lunch was a burger, fries, frozen hot chocolate and a candy cane at Serendipity 3.

"I love this restaurant," he said, as they joined the lineup to the front door across from Bloomingdales.

"So do many other New Yorkers," Noelle commented with a smile.

He laughed. "It's been featured in Hollywood movies and TV shows—that explains it. The food is good, though, too."

"Yes, it is!" proudly proclaimed the server who was passing along the line, taking names for his clipboard.

"Matt Kezanski."

"And Kenneth and Kelsey." Kenneth watched the server as he wrote the names. "And Nonny."

Noelle wondered how she would keep Kelsey entertained during the forty minutes they were told it would take to get a table.

Kenneth would be no problem. He was entranced by a diorama of eight reindeer that seemed to be waiting for Santa and their upcoming epic trip from the North Pole.

"Hey, Kenneth, do you have a fa-vorite?" Matt asked. Nothing but a glare in return.

What was going on with the little guy? Noelle's grandma guilt seemed to be in overdrive today. The little boy already seemed to be a bit upset by the amount of time that his parents had to be away for work reasons. Now he had to share his grandma with this new threat, this stranger?

She knew that if she felt neglected by someone she loved, she'd resent anything or anyone he gave his attention to.

And rightly so. Love and attention are in finite supply in today's busy world. A six-year-old needs more than most and hasn't got the wisdom or resources that a grownup has, to get what he needs. His parents, and if not, his grandma, had to step in to give him time and attention.

Anybody . . . especially Matt . . . had to accept that.

They inched ahead and Noelle tried to imagine, optimistically, that they were quite a bit closer to the restaurant door than they were an hour ago.

"Where do reindeer come from, Kenneth?" Matt suddenly asked.

Noelle was startled by the question and Kenneth seemed to be, too.

"I don't know," he said. His voice was surly, but he couldn't take his eyes away from the very lifelike figures on the display.

"What do you think?" Matt seemed interested, but, totally easy with whichever way the answer went.

"I think maybe the North Pole."

Matt nodded. "Me, too."

"Or the South Pole!" Kelsey sang out. "Nonny, is there a South Pole?"

"There is," Noelle confirmed. "But not an East Pole or a West Pole. Why is that, Matt?"

He grinned at her, and she could feel the spark. "Now, don't you put me on the spot, ma'am."

"Where does this 'ma'am' business come from, anyway? Are you from the South?"

"One grandma from South Carolina."

"Aah."

Kenneth looked back and forth between them, and Noelle could feel his pout starting up again.

"Oh, look, here comes the server! Maybe it's our turn," she said.

"It is indeed, Mrs. Kezanski." The man carried a clipboard. "Very close, anyway. Five more minutes, I'd say."

Noelle didn't bother to correct him. It hardly mattered. But just hearing the words was weird. She was Ms. Moran, had been for years. The Mrs. thing was such a quagmire. Why did people assume anything about marital status, ever?

Noelle's phone buzzed. Daisy's name and face were on the call display. Noelle didn't really feel like talking to her, but she supposed that the moment would arrive sooner or later. May as well be now.

"Daisy, hi. What a nice surprise to have you in New York. How are Frost and Trevor?"

"They're fine, Mom. Excited to see you later on today. What are you doing now?"

'Just going for lunch, then more touring the city. Then the Radio City Christmas show."

"Oh, you got tickets! I've heard those are like gold. What time?"

"We couldn't get enough for everybody, Daisy. Just for the four of us."

"You and Georgia and the kids?" Daisy's tone was tense.

"Georgia and Kyle are at work. Me and Matt and the kids."

"Matt? Who is Matt?"

"A new friend that I've made here. He's been showing us around the city yesterday and today and he brought us to this last-minute ticket office. We tried to get Nutcracker tickets, but they were sold out. Months ago, they said. But the Radio City show will be fabulous, I'm sure. Spectacular, I've heard." Noelle grinned at Matt as they moved a few feet closer to the restaurant door.

A Santa's elf had appeared at the head of the line, an open cookie tin in her hand. She bent over the little ones. They all looked starry-eyed, as if they'd suddenly been given an opportunity to meet with a princess.

Kelsey's eyes shone as she stepped forward to take a cookie, her whole body seeming to vibrate with excitement over meeting a real, live elf.

"Daisy, sweetie, I have to ring off," Noelle said. "We're in a lineup for the restaurant and it's almost our time to go in. The kiddies are starving! I'm sorry I couldn't get tickets for you but I'm sure you and Frost and Trevor will find something to do today. Maybe we'll see you tonight at the hotel?"

Noelle probably should have checked with Georgia before issuing that invitation, but no matter what she did, when both Georgia and Daisy were involved, it always seemed to end in fireworks. She'd long ago given up trying to predict what might set them off.

Matt, bless him, was keeping the two youngsters entertained with a story about the adventures of the reindeer with a sore foot.

When Noelle's phone buzzed a second time, she groaned; she was sucked right into the story, too, and wanted to know what would happen to Larry the lame reindeer. She decided to take the call when she saw Isabel's name on the call display.

"Hey, Izzy, what's up?"

"Got a minute to talk?"

She'd heard Isabel on the phone about a million times since they'd become friends at the age of twelve, and she recognized the gulping sound that meant tears were getting in the way of her words.

"It's not great timing. I'm in a restaurant lineup. But I'll find a quiet place to talk, if you need me now."

"No, I need you to talk freely and you can't do that at a restaurant," Isabel said. "I'll be okay, it's just me and Rob."

"You don't sound okay, and please don't ever say "just me" about yourself. Can I call you back this evening? We'll have a long talk." She listened to Isabel breathing deeply. "Around seven? Or will that be awkward, if he's home?"

"He's never home at seven. Will I call you or will you call me?"

"I'll call you," Noelle said. "Talk soon."

When Noelle got back to the doorway, Matt was at the front of the lineup, talking with the clipboard-carrying server.

"It's our turn!" Kenneth said, grabbing Noelle's hand and eagerly barging in when Matt held the door open for him.

Once they'd checked out all the items placed around the rooms, the four-foot-tall candy canes, the tinsel, and the glitter, Noelle got their orders and had the burgers, hot dogs, and frozen hot chocolate in front of them as quickly as she could.

They were hungry, and it didn't take long for the food and ice cream to disappear. Half an hour later, they were back in Matt's car.

"It's only about a mile, but I figured that was too far to make them walk," Matt said.

Noelle looked out the window, toward St. Patrick's Cathedral. Snowflakes drifted down and the midafternoon light on the streets and sidewalks seemed magical. She felt content, almost bliss-ful.

Maybe it was the afterglow from the hot chocolate.

As they got closer to Rockefeller Center, the pedestrian traffic picked up and the vehicle traffic slowed down. Matt rolled along at about fifteen miles an hour, and the pace seemed just right.

"Come on, Noelle," Matt said. "Even a Vermont girl like you, a New York-hater to the core, has to admit this is very pretty."

"Girl?!" Kenneth said scornfully. "She's not a girl."

"She'll always be a girl," Matt said softly. "Some lucky somebody's girl."

DEVIN AUDRAH

CHAPTER 11

The traffic near Rockefeller Center was almost completely stalled.

"How about if you guys hop out here, I'll find a place to park and meet you inside," Matt said.

"Sounds good," Noelle said, unsnapping her seat belt and turning around to check on whether they had hats, scarves, and mittens ready to go.

"Here are your tickets," Matt said, his eyes on the traffic ahead of him while he reached inside his jacket pocket and pulled out the folder. He even made a move like that look graceful and masculine.

Why is it that there are some things that men do that are just . . . attractive, there's no other way to put it. Noelle had to be honest with herself, though. It wasn't just any man doing that—it was Matt. "Here, I'll hold on to mine. You take the rest. The light's turning red up ahead, you can get out there."

Matt coasted to a stop and Noelle briskly hopped out,

opened the back door, and guided Kenneth and Kelsey out to the sidewalk. She heard a voice.

"Well, we meet again. I'd recognize you anywhere."

She bent down to wrap Kelsey's scarf more firmly around her neck, then straightened up and made full-on eye contact with Dan Keyes. "Have you been following me?"

"Not at all," he said. "Lewis and I are here to get b-roll for another feature on holiday events around town."

A cheerful cameraman toting a lens the size of a tractor tire waved at Noelle.

"But I'm glad I ran into you," Dan said. "It's so great to see a grandma out with her family. How about letting us include you in the piece?"

Noelle shook her head. "I can't talk to you now. We're late. Come on, you guys," she said to the little ones, taking each of their hands and willing a path to open through to the theater doors.

Radio City Music Hall had on its Christmas best, and it was even more impressive than the display at the hotel. Even the department store hadn't shown quite this much red, green, silver, and glitter. Noelle wouldn't have thought that was possible.

The art deco lobby took her breath away. Every doorway was draped in garlands and every pillar hosted a brightly lit wreath. A colossal Christmas tree towered toward the mezzanine, glittering with white lights that seemed like a magic web of stars against the deep red color of the walls.

Both Kenneth and Kelsey had their heads tipped back as far as they would go, and if she weren't determined to monitor them every second of every minute, Noelle would have been doing the same.

Ceilings were often ignored by people, and Noelle thought that was a shame. This one was sensational.

The people were almost as entertaining as the setting. Some were obviously out for a very special matinée: the little girls in velvet and organdy dresses, with their hair in ribbons; the little boys in tiny suits, plaid vests, and shiny shoes.

Their parents or grandparents were also in what was still called "Sunday best" in some places: handsome men in dark suits, well-cut top coats, and silk scarves that probably were of little use against the winter cold, but looked terrific. The women were in black dresses that hung perfectly, accented by truly important jewelry.

A few in the crowd had probably come over from some other Christmas activity or tourist sight, and wore more casual clothes. Maybe they'd picked up last-minute tickets, like Noelle and her bunch.

Everyone had an aura of excitement and to-the-peak anticipation, and when the bells rang to call them into the theater, Noelle felt her insides resonate with the sound. She hadn't expected to be so enthusiastic about this—about anything in New York City, frankly—and she realized she had Matt to thank for it.

She looked around through the throng but couldn't see him and decided that it would be best to get the little ones into their seats and into some sort of mildly confined space. The usher at the doorway shone her flashlight on the tickets and directed them toward the fourth row. Four seats on the aisle.

Noelle settled Kenneth and Kelsey be-fore squeezing past

them toward her spot, leaving the seat at the end of the row for Matt. They perched on the edges of their seats, adding their eager voices to the chatter that filled the hall.

"Nonny, look!" was what she heard, over and over.

These seats were so close to the stage that Noelle could imagine they'd be able almost to wave to the dancers. For a moment, she felt as if she were in a dream, with everyone around them seeming to be just as excited as she was. She could feel the energy building, while Christmas music played over a sound system that was unlike anything she'd ever heard, every note distinct and clear, the bass like a deep, warm bath and the melody like a shower under a Hawaiian waterfall. "*We Wish You a Merry Christmas*", indeed.

Matt came hurrying down the aisle just as the lights were dimming. He flashed her a smile with more than a bit of what she thought was relief in it.

Really? Was he that intent on joining them for every minute of this show? Maybe he was just one of those men who hates to arrive late at anything. Or one of those who didn't want to risk not getting in and wasting the money he spent on a ticket.

Maybe it wasn't relief at all. Maybe it was triumph at successfully beating the New York traffic, finding a parking space, and getting to his seat before the opening chords. Noelle looked across the darkened theater at his profile.

On stage, the red curtain rose, there was a round of applause, and she gave her attention to the show. The orchestra started into "*Happy Holidays*". The star in the spotlight was a white harp, twice as large as the woman playing it. About fifty singers walked out from the wings, spreading across the stage and into the aisles.

Even though the light was dim, she could see that Kenneth and Kelsey were mesmerized. It reminded Noelle of the old time TV shows from the '60s and '70s variety shows, mostly gone now, but living on again in this Broadway-style Christmas spectacular.

Both Kelsey and Kenneth sat like little tin soldiers on the edges of their seats, backs straight, eyes wide. All around, the children dressed in their holiday best waited, and the atmosphere of anticipation was palpable.

Matt had told Noelle that it was one of the largest theaters in the world, but it wasn't size that captivated her. It was the sense of luxury and abundance that overflowed, in every detail, from the seats to the stage to the beautiful programs.

Suddenly, the lights went completely down. The music went up, and dancers dashed onto the stage. The Radio City Rockettes were dressed in identical candy cane costumes, sparkly silver stripes alternating with red.

How many were there? Noelle was just trying to count when Matt leaned forward across the two children between them. "How many do you think there are?"

"I got forty the first time and forty-five the second."

"Shh!" directed a prematurely aged ten-year-old behind them. As if the band's rendition of "*Sleigh Ride*" couldn't drown out a few whispers.

Matt had mentioned over lunch that these tickets went on sale every year in February and that they'd only managed to get them because some kind soul had made the effort to turn in two pair that they couldn't use.

"Are they all twins?" Kelsey wanted to know.

Adorable. Noelle made a mental note to define 'twins' for her a bit more precisely when they could talk freely again.

The dancers' precision was amazing—every kick, every move, every smile, perfectly synchronized. And were they really all the same height? They certainly looked it.

The finale of the number was a dazzling display of athleticism. They took their bows, smiled brilliantly at the audience, and ran off into the wings.

"Are they coming back?" Kelsey demanded to know.

"Shh!" The girl in front of them twisted in her seat and hissed in their direction.

The Rockettes returned almost instantly, dressed all in brown with reindeer antlers. Matt was impressed. "I think they changed in under two minutes."

"Shh!" interjected their personal behavior monitor.

"I think it was about a minute," Noelle said. "What do you think happens if they're not ready to go?"

"Shh! Shh!"

Obviously, they were not going to get away with conversation here. They watched the rest of the number in silence and applauded enthusiastically when the Rockettes ran off the stage.

"Kenneth, tell you what," Matt said. "You change places with me."

In a moment, he and Noelle were seated together, with a child on each side. Noelle took Kelsey's hand firmly in hers.

"Is that another new costume?" Matt whispered into Noelle's ear as the dozens of dancers returned, this time making lines of uniforms.

Noelle nodded. "Let's keep count."

The dancers launched into "*Parade of the Wooden Soldiers*". It was a melody that was very familiar to Noelle. She recalled the times when Georgia and Daisy were little and every favorite song was played so many million times that they all knew every word by heart. They loved these classics and they loved the jingles from the television shows.

"I've seen the costumes in photos from the '30s," Matt said. "They haven't changed."

The set décor was just as dazzling as the costumes. When the Christmas tree number began, Kelsey whispered to Noelle, "That's my favorite!"

A few minutes later, Matt's hand made its way over into Noelle's lap to take hers in his. She inhaled involuntarily. It felt so right.

"How long is the show?" Noelle whispered to him.

"About ninety minutes," Matt said. "Do you think the kids will last that long?"

"I hope so," she said. "I'd like to see it all."

The Living Nativity scene brought a quiet tone to the hall, as the program now made it clear that this season was about the birth of Jesus. Noelle didn't know whether Georgia and Kyle had a visit to church planned as part of this trip, or whether to suggest it, but at least these few minutes in the theater were giving the season some meaning.

The sheep, donkeys, and camels that were part of the story had Kenneth and Kelsey enthralled. "Are they alive?" Kelsey asked, her eyes the size of dinner plates.

Noelle smiled at Matt and squeezed his hand. He'd made this all possible for them to see. "I think these kiddies are here for the duration," Noelle said to Matt.

And they were, with Kelsey announcing each number as her new favorite as soon as it was done. During the rag dolls number, she was on the edge of her seat, watching the dancers tap their way through the intricate moves. Noelle couldn't get over the sounds of their shoes filling every corner of the hall.

"They must have microphones at ground level!" she said to Matt.

"In their shoes," he replied. "In the heels."

Just when Noelle thought she couldn't be any more fascinated, the stage turned into a skating rink.

Watching the dancers become skaters, Noelle remembered her moments on the ice at Central Park with Matt. Could it be true that it was only two days ago? She felt as though she'd been with him a very long time.

The tap dancing was soon over-shadowed, in Kelsey's opinion, by the dancing Santa's. Her little head nodded up and down in time to the music and followed the line of dancers across the stage.

"Is that the North Pole?" she wanted to know, right before giving that number her first-prize badge as the new favorite.

Then, an usher appeared at the right end of Noelle's row of seats, handing out 3-D cardboard glasses. Kelsey was entranced with the task of taking several pairs from the woman sitting to her right and handing them over to her grandmother, Matt, and then Kenneth. "What are these for?" she asked.

"Put them on, honey," Noelle said. "I think we'll need them to see the next number."

"I don't see anything!" Kenneth complained as the glasses slid down his nose.

"Hang on a few minutes, buddy," Matt said. "There's more coming."

And indeed, there was. Noelle held her breath, just as overwhelmed as the little ones were, as they watched Santa's sleigh rise and fly over the stage. Her mood continued through the singing of *"Hark the Herald Angels Sing"*, the angels' costume colors giving the appearance of an oil painting.

On the way out, Matt was waiting for her review. "Well?"

She smiled and squeezed his hand once more, before letting go. She wanted to return to 'grandma' role for the benefit of the grandchildren. "Well, I've seen quite a few holiday shows in my time, but that has to be the best one." Matt beamed at her, but she wasn't finished. "Except for The Nutcracker. That's my favorite."

Matt made a face at her. "You're tough."

She was in the middle of laughing at him and thinking up a retort when she spotted Dan Keyes mingling with the crowd on the sidewalk outside the theater. "Oh no," she said to Matt. "It's that TV reporter from the other day."

Matt read her expression and stepped forward. His own face had a rather unreadable expression: annoyed? Taking over? He looked as if this wasn't an unfamiliar situation for him. "Mr. Keyes! Is there something I can do for you?"

The TV reporter looked him up and down, then smiled. What was that, a smirk? A challenge? "Noelle's daughter, Georgia, told me I might find her here, and I waited to catch you after the performance. I hope you all enjoyed the show. Can I speak with you, Noelle, for a minute?"

"I just have to make a call first," she said, walking away

from him toward a quiet, open spot in front of the pawn-shop next door. She punched Georgia's number into her phone.

"I did not say okay to this!" she said as soon as Georgia answered the phone.

"And I did not say it was okay for you to spend so much time with this Matt guy. Is that his name? Who is he, anyway? Mom, this is New York. You have to be careful."

"I don't remember agreeing to ask your permission."

"Well, they're my children! Not yours. And where are you? Pamela is here at the hotel, Mom, waiting to take them out for supper."

"They're hungry now, and we're going to get them something to eat right next door. Pamela can see them when we get there."

"When will that be?"

"By six, I think."

"Daisy and Trevor are coming over at seven."

"We'll be back right after we eat."

Noelle could feel Georgia searching for something to say. "What are you going to feed them?"

Noelle laughed. "Come on, Georgia. You can't drive a car unless you're willing to be the one behind the wheel."

When she got back to her group outside the Radio City Music Hall door, Matt and Dan faced each other across about ten feet of sidewalk, both with arms crossed. Kenneth and Kelsey were gobbling up hot dogs, big smears of mustard decorating their chins. Those were as big a hit as Noelle would have expected. "Mommy doesn't let us have hot dogs," Kenneth said as he wolfed his down, allowing Noelle to mop the mustard from his chin.

"Did you both say 'thanks' to Mr. Kezanski?" Noelle asked.

"I'm supposed to call him Mr. Matt," Kenneth informed her. "And yes, we did."

Noelle turned to Dan. "Mr. Keyes, we're going back to our hotel now. I'll call you tonight after I've discussed this with my daughter and let you know my decision, as I told you earlier today that I would. Please don't call my daughter again," she said as formally as she could.

"Yes, of course, Ms. Moran," Dan said.

Somehow, as she rode back to the hotel, Noelle wasn't confident that he wasn't on the phone to Georgia again, right then.

The scene behind the hotel suite door was chaotic. Georgia and Kyle were both on their phones; Trevor and Frost were watching cartoons, the volume level up loud enough to entertain the guests next door; and Daisy was motoring around the hotel suite, fussing about something.

"She rarely sits down, that girl," Noelle whispered to Matt as she hung their coats in the closet by the door.

He grinned at her. "Thanks for inviting me up," he said. "How many relatives do I have to see all at one time?"

Noelle stopped to count. "You've got Georgia and Kyle, Daisy and Trevor, their little boy, Frost. Kenneth and Kelsey. So that's seven."

"Make that eight." Pamela's voice behind Noelle was low and confident. In the years Noelle had known her, she'd never seen Pamela anything less than ready to stand in the front row.

Noelle turned around just in time to see Pamela reach

past her, hand extended to take Matt's. Her other hand reached out and enclosed his. "Nice to meet you . . . ?"

"Matt." His face didn't look that friendly, but he was obviously relaxed, and willing to stop whatever he was doing to respond to Pamela's hello.

Pamela seemed to be swaying slightly as she looked Matt over. Perhaps that only existed in Noelle's head? Now, she came to a full stop and stared into his eyes. "Matt? Matt Kezanski? The man who runs St. Mary's Hospital?

Matt looked rather uncomfortable. "Yes, I guess so. Well, previously, anyway. I've just retired."

Pamela turned to Noelle. "You probably wouldn't know this, since you come from Vermont"—she said the word as if it were the same distance as Mars—"but the Kezanski family owns three of the major department stores in New York."

Hmm. Did that explain why a light suddenly seemed to have gone on in Pamela's face?

"Georgia tells me you all saw the Radio City Christmas Spectacular today."

"And it was," Matt said. "Spectacular. We thought we might see the Nutcracker Ballet, but those tickets weren't available."

Pamela nodded. "They are hard to get. Mine are in the third row."

"That's wonderful, Mom," Kyle said. "I'm glad you were able to get the tickets. I know how much you were looking forward to it. When do you go?"

"Tomorrow afternoon," Pamela said. "I was just about to tell you all about it. Shall we?"
She guided them all toward the white couches and dropped

herself into a spot beside the fireplace. "I have tickets for Kelsey and Kenneth, too."

"The ballet?" Kenneth caught the word. "The one with the soldier prince and the magician?"

Pamela laughed. "That's the one. Sounds like your mommy has been telling you about it."

"Nonny did," Kenneth said. "She loves the Nutcracker."

Pamela took this moment to savor a little more of her white wine. Noelle felt compelled to fill in the silence.

"Yes, you're right, Kenneth, I do. Ever since my grandma took me to see a performance way back when."

"I'm sorry you won't be able to see the New York version," Pamela said. "But at least the grandchildren will have that pleasure."

Was she ever going to leave? Noelle sat and stewed while Pamela chatted with Matt about city politics and country getaways.

Their phone calls at an end, Georgia and Kyle joined them on the couches. Georgia immediately picked up on the welcome that Pamela was giving Matt. Noelle wasn't sure she was happy about that, but at least it meant that Georgia and Kyle weren't watching Matt for signs of a serial killer or con man past.

"Tell me, Matt, what are your plans for retirement?" Pamela asked.

"Nothing I can really talk about, Pamela," he said, rather formally. "I don't know why, but when my last day arrived it felt like a surprise to me. I don't plan to play golf or travel the world—I've done as much of that as I want to, actually. But I was ready to leave the hospital. The retail business doesn't interest me, so I guess I can say I know what I don't want, but I don't know what I do want." The words were downbeat, but Matt's smile seemed relaxed. "I'm just hanging out in my condo, waiting for the right thing to come along."

"Maybe it's mentoring that you'd like to do," Kyle suggested.

"Maybe," Matt said. "What is it that you do, Kyle?"

Kyle told the saga of the toy company. It was the first time Noelle had heard it presented, elevator-pitch style. Given that it was New York, where the elevator rides go on a lot longer, there was quite a bit of information.

But she was impressed and she could see that Matt was, too; at least, she hoped he was. If he was bored or put off, he was very skillful at concealing it.

"Nonny, are we going to do something?" Kenneth was becoming restless. Noelle actually thought the little ones had done very well at sitting quietly and listening to the adults for as long as they had.

"Would you like to read a book with me?" she said.

Matt leaned forward and reached into his jacket pocket. "Or maybe you'd like to add these ornaments that I bought for your tree this afternoon?"

He pulled out three sturdy, small globes, each painted with an image of a superhero and topped with a red satin ribbon. Kenneth's face lit up, and he held out his hands to take all three, carefully passing one each to Kelsey and to Frost. They scrambled down from the couch and headed over toward the tree.

"When did you have time to get those?" Noelle whispered to him, as she got up to go help the youngsters.

"In between parking the car and the show," Matt said. "I'm glad they like them. Now, where were we? Oh, yes, I was just going to ask you, Trevor, what you and Daisy do."

Trevor's life as an engineer and Daisy's as a piano teacher were given just as much attention as Kyle and Georgia's as manufacturing moguls. Matt was racking up big brownie points.

Everyone was getting along. Noelle knew that at some point this week Georgia and Daisy would clash, but she was pleased it wasn't happening within hours of them arriving in the same zip code for a while.

The kiddies left behind a marathon of holiday cartoons on the TV, as they ran off to be Christmas tree decorators. Noelle heard the channels being changed and when she returned to sit beside Matt, they were all looking at a classic Christmas movie. It was the heartwarming one where the man gets a look at what life in his town would be if he'd never been born. Kenneth and Kelsey began a new game of whispering "cookies" in Noelle's ear every few minutes.

"I have to get going," Pamela said. "I have dinner plans. Matt, is there any chance you're heading my way, over toward the park?"

"I wasn't planning on leaving just yet," Matt said.

Noelle had to hold herself back from yelling "yes" and punching the air.

"We'll see you to the door, Mom," Kyle said. Georgia took her cue and rose to follow them.

Jimmy Stewart confirmed the angels, wings, and bells connection, then Daisy turned off the TV. Kenneth put up a protest. "It's our turn now!"

"Well, Frost is going to do something else for a while," Daisy said. "Trevor, could you help me get him a snack?"

"What'll it be?" Noelle asked as she settled the kiddies onto the couch cushions that Georgia and Daisy had just vacated. "Frost, come on over here and watch a movie with your cousins. *Elf? Rudolph? Charlie Brown?*"

"*The Grinch!*" Kenneth said, squirming down into his spot on the couch.

"You know, there's a holiday movie settings tour of New York that might be fun," Matt said.

"There's a tour of almost everything, somewhere in New York," Noelle said, looking into his eyes and daring him. "You know I love movies and I think you're just trying to get me onside with New York that way. No sale."

"Everybody, I'm on my way." Pamela appeared in the living room, wearing knee-high white boots, a red coat, and a winter hat made of white felt and cut in a shape that Noelle couldn't define but could recognize as quite stylish. "Nice to see you again, Daisy. Matt, it was wonderful to meet you and I hope to run into you again, sometime. Kenneth, Kelsey, I'll pick you up tomorrow at 12:30."

And she was gone. Noelle wasn't sure whether she was insulted or relieved to be ignored. As soon as the door closed behind her, Noelle went over to talk with Georgia, standing by the sideboard with the wine bottles. "She's taking them out tomorrow at 12:30? Are you going along?"

"We have another big day of work tomorrow," Georgia said. "You seem to be quite busy these days," her eyes were on Matt as she said it, "so we jumped at Pamela's offer to take them to the ballet."

"I know she was talking about the ballet, but I didn't quite put it all together," Noelle said. "What will they be doing until she shows up at 12:30? For a two o'clock matinée, I assume."

"She'll pick them up to take them to the performance," Georgia said. "You can enjoy them in the morning."

"And get them ready to go out at 12:30?" Noelle said. "Baths, dressed up in good clothes? Shoes polished? Hair brushed? Kelsey's in braids, maybe a French one?"

Georgia could read Noelle's meaning. "No, never mind. You don't have to do anything, Mom, you don't even have to be here. I can see that you think you have better things to do. I'll ask Daisy."

"Ask my wife what?" Trevor emerged from the bathroom. Clearly, he was making himself at home. He was barefoot now and had his shirttails out, his hair uncombed, and a book in his hand.

His facial expression read 'grumpy' and he barely acknowledged Noelle or her brief introduction to Matt.

After he walked off toward the kitchen, probably to look for something to eat, which was his second-most frequent activity, after TV-watching, Georgia asked Daisy, "What's bugging him?"

"What do you mean?"

"He seems very cranky."

"I don't think so," Daisy said. "Mom, does Trevor seem cranky to you?"

"Don't drag me into it," Noelle said.

"Who's cranky?" Trevor asked. He walked in carrying a sandwich and a canned soda. He popped the top off and dropped it on the coffee table.

Daisy shot him a warning look, but it soon became clear, it did no good.

"If you're talking about me, I confess," Trevor said. "Yes, I admit it. Daisy might not have mentioned it but we had plans for this week, before we got the summons to be here."

"Nobody summoned you to be here," Georgia said. "You just took it upon yourselves to show up."

"Oh, come on," Trevor said. "You made a big deal about a family Christmas. In New York. With Noelle here. The grandkids seeing their cousin. How could we not show up? Daisy won't tell you herself, but she felt pressured."

"Why can't Daisy speak for herself?" Georgia asked.

"You know, I've wondered why so many families today ask older parents to come along on holiday rather than take their own," Noelle said. "I thought, at first, it was because they enjoyed their company. But now I think they are looking for a break from their own children, because grandma and grandpa are so great about giving child care."

"Mom. We thought you'd like to see New York at Christmas. Everybody loves it. And we wanted to see you, spend the holidays with you," Georgia said.

"Did you? Then why didn't you come to visit me in Burlington?"

Georgia looked a bit flustered. "Well, all right, yes. It was sort of . . . Multi-tasking." She read the look on Noelle's face and rushed to say more. "We thought it was important to give you something to do."

Digging herself deeper.

"I think you should consider that I might have something I want to do," Noelle said. She looked over toward Matt, who sat on the couch between Kenneth and Kelsey, an arm around each as they watched the Grinch and Max steal all the presents and trees in Whoville.

Georgia looked at them both, then seemed to decide to speak her mind. "What? Be with a total stranger at the one time of year that's supposed to be all about family?"

"The one time of year?" Noelle asked. "What about Thanksgiving? The Fourth of July? Memorial Day picnic? Easter? Labor Day? Birthdays?" She glanced over her shoulder at Kenneth and Kelsey but they seemed to be oblivious to the tension rising among the adults.

"All right, you're right, Mom, there are plenty of holidays. But we all enjoy them and it's important to get together," Georgia said.

"But maybe there should be a little more democracy about where, and how, and for how long," Daisy said.

Georgia turned to face her. "Are you saying I boss everybody around?"

"I'm saying you have a strong personality and you usually get your way," Daisy refused to be walked backward into a corner. "Mom should be the one choosing what and how we do holidays. She's the …the…"

"The old one?" Noelle laughed, trying to get them to stand down.

"Mom tells me everything about what she's feeling about things, and she's very understanding," Georgia said. "She knows how important this week is to us, for the business, and that's why she agreed to meet us here instead of at home."

That wasn't quite the way Noelle remembered it, but there were enough people in this ring and she wasn't about to climb in, too.

"Mom is very understanding and we're very lucky to have her," Daisy said. "You wouldn't believe the stories I hear from my friends about the things their mothers do."

"Oh, I bet I would. I hear some those stories, too," Georgia said. "Ours is a peach." She reached an arm around Noelle's shoulders and gave her a squeeze.

"She is," Daisy declared, reaching in for her own hug. "But I'm not too sure about this new man friend business."

"I know, right?"

Georgia had a twinkle in her eye, but Noelle didn't like the way this was going. She looked back and forth between the two of them and realized they were teasing her. At least, she hoped so. It was better than listening to them fight.

"Just keep it friendly, Mom."

"What do you mean, Daisy?"

"Come on, Mom," Georgia said. "Fifty-five is too old for romance."

Until yesterday morning, Noelle would have agreed with them.

As the movie wound round to its end, and the Whos stood around the tree singing, Kenneth and Kelsey remembered they had one more mission in mind for this evening.

"Cookies!"

'Nonny, really," Kelsey wheedled. "We have to know what's in the next tin."

"How do you know there is a next tin?"

"You told us! One for every day of the visit."

Noelle went to her suitcase, crammed in the corner of the closet bedroom, and pulled out a gold cookie tin covered in a Christmas tree pattern. "They're called Rice Krispie Mash-ups," she said.

Kelsey's mouth was full of one, instant-ly.

"I think I should get a chance to sample this amazing Christmas baking I've been hearing about," Matt said, reaching for one of the cookies.

Noelle wished she had a chef's kitchen, an entire afternoon, and a refrigerator full of goodies to turn into a feast for him.

"What's in them?" Georgia asked.

"Rice krispie cereal, marshmallows, chocolate chips, raisins, peanut butter, pretzel sticks. And sprinkles."

"I didn't want the recipe, Mom. I wanted to know why you're giving them sugar at this time of night."

"Well, I wanted the recipe," Daisy said. "Thanks, Mom."

"Sucking up, as usual," Georgia said.

And the war was on again.

"Do you want to go down to the lobby for a drink?" Matt was at Noelle's right shoulder, drawing her attention away from the Georgia-and-Daisy show. Drawing her attention away—and letting the air out of the feeling that she always had, that she was responsible for their squabbles and that she was the one who was supposed to resolve them. The peacekeeper, that was her role as a kid and it was the role (one of them) that she'd stepped into as an adult in the family she created.

When she told Matt all this, as they sat in the bar

downstairs with their drinks, he nodded. "I guessed as much," he said. "You looked as though you were about to get mixed up in it and I just didn't want to let that happen."

The music coming from the bandstand at the other end of the bar was a cool mix of jazz, soul, and Christmas standards, all delivered by an inspired piano, a saxophone, and drums. Matt had chosen a table for two as far back in a dim corner as possible, and Noelle felt herself relax as soon as they sat down.

When the server came around, she ordered a hot buttered rum, and Matt went for a Scotch. "Now, tell me who you are," she said. "Why did Pamela perk up like that when you said your name?"

The final chords of a very jazzy version of "Deck the Halls" were just echoing away. Harmonie stepped back from her spot in front of the microphone, her silver lamé dress catching the spotlight in a vision of tinsel. Noelle stood up to get her attention and wave her over to join them.

Harmonie was delighted. "How nice to see y'all here, Miss Noelle! I'd have thought you'd be in bed, asleep, by this time of night," she said with a wink.

"How're things?" Noelle asked.

"Good."

"How's the chef?"

Harmonie smiled. "Good."

"A-ha. Fast work."

"You have to," Harmonie said. "Life is short." But her eyes shifted away from Noelle's and Noelle suddenly had a vibe that all was not going well with the chef. "And who is this?"

"This is Matt. He's a friend, a New Yorker. He's trying to convince me it's not so bad here."

"We're on the same page, then," Harmonie laughed. "I love New York. Especially at Christmas, isn't it wonderful? What places have you been showing her?"

Noelle's phone buzzed and she looked down to see Isabel's name on the call display. Was it really seven o'clock already?

"I'm sorry, but I have to take this. Is it okay if I just duck over there for a while?" she asked, pointing out a beautiful, holly-green armchair across the lobby.

"Of course," Matt said.

"We'll pick up on the details of your checkered career and shady life as soon as I get back," Noelle smiled.

As Noelle had expected, Isabel was not upset, the way she had been when she phoned earlier.

"Come on, Isabel, it's me," Noelle said. "I'm sorry I wasn't available to talk when you called, but I'm here now. What's going on?"

"Nothing I want to talk about. I can fix it by myself."

"Why should you have to?"

Noelle looked around the hotel lobby while she waited out Isabel's silence.

"I think we're going to have to see someone for couples counseling," Isabel said finally. "I don't want to suggest it because he turned me down last time I asked, but it's getting to the point where I think I'll have to push."

"Nothing wrong with that," Noelle said. "But do you mean he actually said no?"

"Well, no, I guess not really. I suggested it and he didn't answer. He says that's not saying no."

"Yes, it is," Noelle said. "It's saying no and it's ignoring you. You shouldn't have to plead or make demands about this. If he values you, and your marriage, he'll go with you."

Wow. She certainly was confident in her opinions about Isabel's situation. Why was it always so much easier to see someone else's solution than your own?

She didn't know whether Isabel's silence meant that she was processing the advice and intending to act on it or that she wanted to change the subject. She'd had these opinions about Rob and the way he treated Isabel for years, and had never had the nerve to bring them out into the open. Now that she and Isabel were finally talking, she decided to take a chance and say what she wanted to say.

"You shouldn't have to guess whether someone you're tied to cares about you."

There.

Noelle thought she could hear Isabel's breathing getting ragged. Had she gone too far?

"I'll think about that, Noelle, I really will," Isabel said. "Let's talk about something else now. How is New York? And the shopping? Have you found those toys you were hunting for?"

"No, I'm still looking," she said. "You'd think they have everything in New York but they don't."

"I put out a few feelers here and I'm keeping a look-out for them," Isabel said. "That's what I really called about today, to tell you that."

It seemed that Isabel was already retreating into her cave, afraid of being out in the open with her thoughts about Rob, and perhaps feeling guilty about being disloyal.

Misplaced loyalty, in Noelle's opinion. But now that they were on to the safer topic of shopping, it just wouldn't be right to make that comment.

"Thanks, Izzy, that would be great."

"You take care, and we'll see you when you get back."

When Noelle shut off the call and walked back toward the table, she saw that Matt and Harmonie now had a third person sitting with them—Dan Keyes.

"You seem to turn up almost everywhere I go," she commented.

"I turn up a lot of places a lot of people go," he countered.

Noelle picked up on an atmosphere of tension around the table. What had Dan said? Or was it Matt?

"And I'm sure you're welcome wherever that is."

It was Matt, and the tone was about as sarcastic as it gets.

"I heard you tell the cab driver at the airport where you were staying, remember?" Dan said. "I was in the neighborhood and I thought I'd stop in to find out what fantastic place you have on your agenda for tomorrow." He stood up. "But I just got a call and I have to go. My offer still stands, Noelle. Let me know."

CHAPTER 12

That Wednesday morning, the fantastic place on Noelle's agenda was the skating rink at Bryant Park. Ever since the kiddies heard that their grandma had gone skating, they wanted to try. The rink there was not as busy as Central Park's, Matt said, and the crowds there were less frantic than in the stores.

For a while, it looked as though Daisy, Trevor, and Frost would accompany them to Bryant Park to skate, but at the last minute, Trevor put his foot down and said that since he was spending his pre-Christmas week in New York having no say in the decision, he wanted to be the one choosing their activities. And today, he wanted to see Yankee Stadium, even though it would be covered in snow.

"What about you, Daisy?" Noelle asked. "Would you and Frost like to spend the morning with us at Bryant Park?"

"I think Trevor would prefer if we stay with him," Daisy said. "But thanks for the invite, Mom."

So, Noelle bundled up Kenneth and Kelsey. She made sure they were well-equipped for the December weather but, as she shepherded them into a taxi and a blast of cold air whipped across her face, she was regretting the rush to get ready to leave on the plane four days ago.

So many things she'd forgotten to bring, but the most annoying was the warm scarf.

"There is no place in New York that isn't jam-packed," Noelle said to Matt as they lined up for skates.

"Haven't I shown you enough yet for you to overlook that?" he asked.

"There probably just aren't enough sights to see for me to get to that point." Noelle led him and the two little ones along to the bench where they could change out of their shoes.

"Look at you shivering," Matt commented as he kneeled beside her, tying Kenneth's skate laces.

"I know. I'm just kicking myself, that I didn't think to bring a scarf."

Matt reached up toward the scarf around his neck and she saw that he was wearing two. He unwrapped one of them and put it over her head, circling it twice around her neck.

"Oh, no, Matt, I couldn't."

"Of course, you could. I've watched you all week, shivering away, and I couldn't stand it another minute. Think of it as an early Christmas gift."

Noelle's heart turned over. Literally.

It was a beautiful shade of turquoise, not his color at all. Why fight it? She gave in.

Kenneth and Kelsey loved the skating just as much as Noelle expected, and it was a golden morning. Everyone was laughing, including Kelsey, when her feet went out from under her and she landed on her little tush.

After they skated, they wandered around the stalls at the Christmas market. Kelsey wanted to buy a gift for her mother. Noelle doubted the red sweater with reindeer antlers would be well-received, or worn very often, but she supported Kelsey's choice. She didn't want Kelsey to grow up letting other people's opinions be her guidance system.

"We have to have them back by noon at the latest," Noelle said. "Pamela is coming to pick them up for the ballet at 12:30."

"Are you very disappointed that you won't be seeing the Nutcracker while you're here?" Matt asked.

"Yes and no," Noelle said. "But I'm having a great time this week, so it doesn't matter."

"Well, how about having a better one?" Matt said, reaching into his jacket pocket. "Merry Christmas."

In his gloved hand, he held out a ticket with a photograph of the Sugar Plum Fairy. For a moment, Noelle felt it hard to catch her breath.

"Where did you get that?"

"Robbed a bank, ma'am," he said. "It was a box office, actually."

"It's for me? But I don't think I could . . . " What she couldn't do was take her eyes off it.

"What else will you be doing this afternoon? Watching TV? Baking cookies? Yes, it's for you."

Her smile was as wide as the East River. "New York is magic."

"I thought you said New York sucked," Matt said.

"It does have some advantages."

"A little culture."

"And some delightful men," Noelle added.

"Some? Or one in particular?"

"You," she agreed.

Wait a minute, what's going on here?

Matt reached for her hand, opened it, and laid the ticket in her palm.

Noelle stared down at the gift. "You're a good friend."

"I don't want to be a friend," he said, smiling.

"I'm too old for anything else," No-elle said.

"No, you're not," he insisted. "You're fifty-five. You've barely got started."

"The grandkids need me."

"Not all the time. Not your whole life."

After Matt dropped them off at the hotel, Noelle hustled the kiddies through the lobby. They were running short of time, if she was to have them ready for the other grandmother by 12:30. She almost didn't break stride when she crossed paths with Harmonie in front of the elevator.

But then she saw the young woman's face. She was upset.

"What is it, Harmonie?" she said. "What's wrong?"

Harmonie rubbed at her eyes and took a deep breath.

"It's nothing, Noelle," she said. "Just some friction with the management here."

Noelle had a feeling it went deeper. "Ride up with us," she said. "I have to get the kids dressed to go out, but we can talk until we get there. Have to get myself ready for the ballet, too, but I have no idea what I'm going to wear."

It took only ten seconds and the closing of the elevator door for Harmonie to open up. "They object to me spending time with Justin," she said. "There, I said it out loud. I've been trying to be cool, let on like it doesn't matter, but it does!"

"What happened, exactly?"

"The hotel manager called me in for a meeting this morning, and I thought it had something to do with the setlist for the show or something special for the Christmas Buffet event or something. I get there, and the restaurant manager is there, and the events coordinator and the concierge."

"Donald?"

"Yeah, I couldn't quite figure that one out myself. But the others seemed to know so much about Justin and me. I think Donald has been reporting on me."

Kenneth and Kelsey were staring at Harmonie with eyes wide and Noelle realized that this was an adult conversation that she ought to take offline.

"I'm so sorry to hear you're having a bad day." She tried to signal to Harmonie with her eyes that she should tell her story keeping in mind that it was being absorbed by little pitchers with big ears.

Harmonie understood instantly. "I know it will get better. I told my boss that Chef Justin and I will work hard at doing our jobs."

The elevator doors opened on their floor, and Noelle pulled out her keycard for the door.

When she opened it, the sight (and sound) was a five-alarm argument underway between Georgia and Daisy. They had managed to agree that the Dickens Buffet at the hotel on Christmas Eve would be a good choice of an activity for the little ones, but the room was up in flames about what the children would wear.

"If the boys don't want to wear ties, they don't have to!" Daisy said through gritted teeth. "Mom, what do you think?"

"I think it's two days away and why not fight about something that's right here, right now, rather than borrowing Friday's issues?" Noelle said. "Georgia, what are you doing here, anyway? Don't you have a meeting?"

"The meeting this afternoon is online. We've got people connecting from eight different countries, all around the world," she said.

The door was still open. Harmonie stood in the hallway, uncertain about what to do next.

"Yes, can I help you?" Georgia said.

"Georgia, this is my friend, Harmonie," Noelle said. "We're having a conversation but I think we'll have to continue it at another point," she said to Harmonie with a smile. "We have to have the kids ready to go by 12:30 and I have to get myself over to Lincoln Center by 1:30."

"Why? Why are you going over there?" Georgia asked.

"Harmonie, let's talk some more later this afternoon," Noelle said. "I'm interested."

"I'll be around," Harmonie said, her smile back to normal.

"What's the fight about?" Noelle asked as she hung up her coat in the closet. "And by the way, how do we tell what

Frost wants?" Noelle asked, looking at her youngest grand-child, who was chewing on the fabric end of a clip-on tie.

"Even for the smallest ones, it's good training," Georgia said. "If they feel like good clothes are unusual or uncomfortable, they'll want to be sloppy all their lives. This is New York, not Portland or Burlington. If you were going, Daisy, you'd see that all the other little boys there will be dressed up."

Noelle left the two of them debating, and followed the little ones down the hall to the bathroom. A tub full of warm water, some giggles over toys, boats, and mermaids, and then a few rousing choruses of their favorite songs, and everyone was in the best possible mood.

She heard the suite door open and close, followed by Kyle's voice, then an unfamiliar female one. Oh, of course, that was probably Pamela.

She took the kids into their bedroom and helped Kelsey get into her red velvet dress, her white tights, and her black patent shoes. For Kenneth, it was dress gray pants, a white shirt, and a miniature navy blazer, complete with a pocket puff that matched his little tie. Was there much call for this in Cincinnati, or was Georgia on drugs?

She guided them out into the living room, where the adults sat on the couches gathered around the massive teak coffee table.

"Oh, don't you look cute!" Pamela was well turned out herself, in a little black dress, black tights, and black patent pumps.

"Oh, good, I'm glad you're all here," Noelle said. "I didn't get a chance to tell you, Georgia, but I have a ticket to the ballet now, and I'm going to have to get a move on, if I'm going to make it there by two o'clock. I still have to change."

"How did you get a ticket?" Pamela asked.

"Matt," Noelle said, and several eyebrows went up. "Just one, though."

"Yes, it's been sold out for months." Pamela was on her feet. "We'd better get rolling. Kids, get your coats."

"I was wondering if I could catch a ride over with you," Noelle said. "I can get changed real quick."

"I'm sure you can, but I'm sorry, no, Noelle, you can't go with us," Pamela said. "We don't have room."

"Kyle could drive you and I could stay back here at the hotel," Georgia said. "Mom could sit in the back with the kids."

"Oh no, Georgia, you don't need to do that," Noelle said.

"It's fine, Mom, I'd like to. I have some work to get done and I could use the extra hour," Georgia said.

Kyle had an opinion, though. "This is a special occasion that my mom organized," he said to Georgia. "I want you, her, and my kids in the car. We'll get a cab over for your mom."

Noelle had not realized this had the potential to turn into a problem. "That will be just fine. I don't want to be a bother. I'll get a taxi."

Georgia looked toward the windows, where they could see that the snow was coming down hard again. "That might not be easy."

"Oh, it will be okay, Georgia. New York has plenty of taxis," Noelle said. "And a few other things."

"So, you're starting to lighten up on your opinion

about New York," Pamela said.

"There are a few things I'm liking, yes," Noelle admitted. "The harbor is wonderful and the street food is fantas-tic."

"And the Christmas show!" Kenneth had decided to tune in on this conversation.

"With the lady dancer elves!" Kelsey chimed in.

Kyle's cell phone buzzed and he glanced at the screen. "I have to take this," he said, disappearing toward the main bedroom. Georgia fussed over straightening Kenneth's lapels.

A knock at the suite door was the final straw in breaking up their discussion of New York's charms.

Noelle opened it to find a bellhop standing there, holding some sort of garment under plastic.

"Georgia?" she called over her shoulder. "Did you send something out for dry cleaning?"

No answer from the living room. Noelle reached out for the hanger, but before he gave it to her, the bellhop handed her an envelope with a note.

Maybe you didn't bring anything really fancy? This is one of my favorites. It's one-size-fits-all, so it should be okay. The shoes aren't my taste, but Chloe in the kitchen had a pair. H.

When Noelle got the hanger back to her nook, she pulled the plastic off a black, knee-length wrap dress with a Milky Way of sequins and glitter around the neckline. Understated but special. Much too much for a Wednesday afternoon in Vermont, but just right for a show in New York. *Oh, Harmonie, thank you!*

Noelle pulled off her sweater and pants, did a quick spritz of cologne, then slipped on the dress. Just fine. On with the low-heeled black pumps, a comb through her hair, and a bit of lip-stick, and she was ready to go.

She arrived back in the living room just in time to hear Pamela saying, "All right, everybody, time to go. Let's make sure we give ourselves lots of time to get there."

They stared at Noelle's outfit but she ignored their curiosity, waving goodbye to Daisy, Trevor, and Frost and heading for the elevator with Georgia, Kyle, and their kids.

They rode down in silence, then set out across the lobby for the revolving door to the street. Noelle caught sight of herself in the floor-to-ceiling mirrors. Not bad, even for somebody fifty-five.

That was odd. Mirrors in this lobby? She hadn't noticed them before now.

As they walked toward the street, a man in a dark suit, white shirt, and tie, holding a sign that said "Moran", stepped forward. His mustache was from the '70s, and his chubby cheeks were clearly a gift from a long line of people who know how to make pizza.

"Ms. Moran? Your car is out front."

"My car?"

"Mr. Kezanski booked a ride for you, to and from Lincoln Center. He said it would be a surprise, and that I was to give you his card. That you might not trust me." She could see a smile teasing at the edge of his mouth. "You can trust me."

"What's this?" Georgia and Kyle came over to Noelle and the driver.

"Matt sent a car to take me to the theater."

"Why?" Kyle asked. "What's with this guy?"

Noelle saw Pamela give her a measuring sort of look. "That's just wonderful," she said. "Now, it all works out for everyone and no one is talking about taking taxis."

They walked out of the hotel and the driver motioned Noelle toward a new Mercedes, parked in a prime spot just steps from the door.

"I want to go with Nonny Noelle in this car," Kenneth announced.

"Well, you're not doing that," Kyle said. "It's just a short walk to where our car is parked."

"Kyle, let's get the valet to bring it around," Georgia said.

"But that will take longer—oh, al-right." Kyle was not a happy camper.

"I still want to know why he's doing this for you," Georgia said to Noelle.

Pamela smiled at them both, a smile with teeth but no eyes. "I think he's met someone he likes," she said. "Relax, Georgia. He's a good name to know."

No, he's not. Noelle felt a flash of anger. What was that about? Maybe he was a good name to know, but that wasn't even the beginning of what he was.

**

Noelle settled into her seat at Lincoln Center as Tchaikovsky's sublime music filled the air. Oh, sure, she enjoyed a good country tune from time to time, but classical music like this was a sublime crème brûlée, next to a banana pudding.

The curtain rose on a scene straight out of a dream. Noelle had seen this ballet about two dozen times since she was a tiny child. She'd never taken the opportunity to become much of a dance fan. Ian didn't enjoy it at all, not even at Christmas time, and she'd never been able to convince him to accompany her to watch The Nutcracker. She'd gone with a girlfriend a few times and then had tried to turn it into a tradition with Daisy and Georgia, but once they'd moved to other cities and to their own lives, it had been impossible to keep it going and gradually, she let it go.

So many things about her daughters now were only memories from their childhoods and their middle school years. Sometimes, she felt she barely knew them. Did it take daily contact to feel close? Would it be any different if she lived in the same city and just a ten-minute drive away?

She scanned the rows of children and their parents in front of her. The little girls wore velvet dresses and ribbons in their hair, the little boys had vests and jackets with their pants, and tiny clip-on ties on their white shirts. All of them were silent and totally focused on the performance. She was seated in the seventh row and the dancers on the stage seemed close enough to touch.

The opening overture filled the theater, the curtain rose, and the story began, with the Christmas Eve party, the amazing Christmas tree, and the arrival of Drosselmeyer, with his gifts of life-sized dolls and a Nutcracker toy. The Christmas tree grew, the Mouse King arrived to fight, the Nutcracker became a prince, and then it was time for intermission.

Noelle wasn't sure why this ballet en-tranced her the

way it did, year after year; maybe it was the music, maybe the costumes, or maybe the artistry of the dancers.

She couldn't help but notice that in this story from the 1890s, the lovers were young. Lovers are young everywhere, she thought: books, movies, songs, even 18th century ballets and 16th century fairy tales.

But why? Older people fall in love, too. Noelle had the proof of her own experience. She felt it; she knew it. She had had Matt on her mind non-stop now for two days, and she doubted the feeling would go away.

Noelle had told Kelsey that they could see one another at the intermission. As Noelle walked into the lobby, she heard someone calling, "Nonny Noelle! Nonny Noelle!" and she spotted Kelsey halfway up the steps to the balcony.

You had to laugh—it was so adorable.

But Pamela didn't think it was funny. When Noelle got to the staircase, Pamela let her have it, both barrels.

"Look, Noelle, I don't appreciate this."

"I don't know what you're talking about."

"This is my turn to spend time with my grandchildren. You've had them since Saturday."

"There's nothing wrong with both of us being here."

"Yes, there is. You're distracting them," Pamela said. "I didn't interfere while you were looking after them."

"You could have had them any one of those days. Or for a few hours on each. Whatever you wanted, whatever was convenient for you. That's what you did anyway. They've been available to you all those other hours, and it would have been a big help to Georgia and Kyle if you'd pitched in—"

"Not to mention, to you! It would have given you

more hours to spend with your new flame."

"Again, I don't know what you're talking about. I've been here since Saturday. I'm helping to look after my grandchildren, and you're welcome to do the same. Kelsey, Kenneth, I'll have to see you back at the hotel at suppertime." Noelle turned to walk away and Pamela darted to the left, to stand in her path.

"You're out of your league, Noelle," Pamela said. "A man like that. In his sixties, just widowed, not working an eighty-hour week anymore, not frozen into being a grumpy old man—they'll be lining up for him."

"I don't compete for men," Noelle said. Where had that come from? She hadn't said anything, or had a thought like that, since the '80s. "If he's going to call me, he'll call me. Or not."

"He won't," Pamela said, stepping aside. "Teenagers do this sort of stuff, not us."

Throughout the second act of the ballet, Noelle couldn't concentrate. The Nutcracker Prince took Clara to the Land of Sweets, the Sugar Plum Fairy wove her magic, and Clara's dream came to an end, but Noelle rode along on the story thanks to memory, rather than present-moment pleasure.

When she walked out into the courtyard in front of Lincoln Center, drifts of snow had turned the scene into something from Currier and Ives. Noelle's head was filled with incredible music and visions of Sugar Plum fairies and Nutcracker princes; she felt strengthened and ready to deal with whatever crap Pamela wanted to deal out.

The car and driver zipped her back to the hotel, and

she was a bit sorry that the ride went by so fast. She hoped that there had been enough time for Pamela to say her good-byes and go home. There's no predicting or controlling the traffic.

Fast as it was, though, she had time to take out her phone and send a text to Matt.

Thank you again for the ballet ticket. It was unbelievable!

She dithered for a few minutes over choosing an emo-ji: what emotion did she want to show him? Was he one of those who preferred letters and punctuation only, and thought that using emojis was lazy or juvenile? She knew she was over-thinking it, and decided to leave it at a simple, old-fash-ioned exclamation mark.

His reply came back in ten seconds.

I'm thrilled. Thank you for letting me give it to you.

A few minutes later, her phone buzzed again.

What are you doing now?

Riding in the car going back to the hotel.

Would you like to meet me for a drink? Maybe a nice dinner?

Noelle stared through the window at the brightly lit store windows as they passed by. What should she do? What did she want to do? She gave herself about five minutes before feeling that she had to give a reply. He must be wondering why the long gap between texts.

Thanks, Matt, but I really have to get back. I've been away all afternoon. And I'd like to hear what the Ks thought of the ballet.

It was his turn to go silent for a few minutes.

Enjoy.

Now, what did that mean?

On her way through the lobby, she saw Harmonie performing by the grand piano, crooning her way through a Christmas standard. There was still a dangling thread on this day—she hadn't thanked Harmonie for the loan of the dress and the shoes. Noelle detoured and dropped herself into a seat at a stage-side table. When the server came by, she decided to treat herself to a glass of wine. She wasn't sure why but something was just off-balance and low; maybe wine would help.

She waited to the end of Harmonie's set, then motioned her over. "Can you join me in a glass of wine? Or would that get you in more trouble with management?" She added a wink of conspiracy to her question but then realized that it was just too soon to joke about this.

Harmonie sat down, leaned back, crossed her legs, and took over. "Wine is a stellar idea. I don't care what they think, you know. It's none of their business. It is just outrageous, the way they've been tracking me!"

"What do you mean?"

"I mean, tracking me! You know, if the boss thinks he should talk to me, privately, about getting into a relationship with Justin, about implications for staff morale, the tone of the place, or the opinions of guests, whether the relationship lasts or it doesn't. But to watch me for weeks, keep spreadsheets about my comings and goings and how they mesh with Justin's, make reports, cross-examine my band mates, call me into a meeting with four other people there! It's just twisted.'

"I agree," Noelle said. "No wonder you're so ticked off."

"I'm ready to quit! I mean, it's been an awesome gig, otherwise. I never thought when I started out back on the block, taking piano lessons and voice lessons and dance lessons, that I'd be a singer in a hotel as fancy as this. Oh sure, I'm like lots of other girls, I had my dreams of Broadway, but I know the odds. And it was tough enough, getting this far. I've had stuff happen and it wouldn't surprise me if I never get to Broadway, but I don't think it would be right to get pushed out of this spot because of my choice of a boyfriend! I mean, come on!"

Noelle felt there was nothing to say at that point.

The server arrived with two glasses of red wine on a tray.

Harmonie barely paused for breath. "Thank you, Katie. This looks so good. And thank you, Ms. Moran, I really appreciate it."

"Please. Call me Noelle."

"It's because you're a guest," Harmonie sipped her wine and smiled. "It's drummed into you in a lot of hotels when you work there, that the first-name basis with guests is off-limits."

"So, I'm just a guest?"

Harmonie smiled. "Yeah, you're not. You're a friend."

"And I want to thank you for what you did for me earlier today. That dress was absolutely perfect. And shoes, too!"

"Did your date like it, too?"

"He wasn't there. He could only get one ticket."

"And he gave it to you," Harmonie said. "My, my."

Noelle grinned back at her. "Yes, I'd say there is something happening here."

"I'd say so."

"But let's get back to you, Harmonie. What happened after they talked to you in the meeting? And I'm so sorry, by the way, that we got interrupted this afternoon."

"That's all right, I get it. So, the manager told me they want me to break it off with Justin. Completely. Not, 'don't be obvious' or 'don't let it interfere with your performance', just 'break it off'. Why? 'Because we say so.' 'It's for the good of the hotel.' Total garbage!"

"Total garbage," Noelle agreed. "What does Justin say?"

"I haven't told him."

"You haven't told him? You have to tell him!"

Harmonie sipped in silence for a few minutes.

"I should have asked you this to start with." Noelle said. "Do you want me to just listen or to give you my advice?"

Harmonie smiled. "Okay, what would you do?"

"I'd tell Justin, first of all. It affects his life as much as yours, and if you just drop him, he'll always wonder what he did wrong. After that, it depends on how he reacts—and what you two decide is the best thing to do. And what you feel like you want to do. Those aren't always the same thing."

"Yeah, I feel you on that." Harmonie looked a lot less stressed than she had when she first sat down. "So, I'll talk it over, first thing."

"Somewhere away from the hotel," Noelle said.

Harmonie nodded, thoughtfully. "Yeah. What crummy timing, though. Tomorrow is the Christmas Eve Buffet, his biggest event of the year. I don't want to interfere with that, or rattle him. The day after is Christmas. Who wants to talk about breaking up relationships on Christmas? But if I leave it 'til after, he might feel like I kept a secret on him."

"Tell him today," Noelle said. "He can handle it. His Buffet will go just fine."

Harmonie stood up and reached toward Noelle for a hug. "Thank you."

"Don't mention it," Noelle said. "But I would like to know what happens."

DEVIN AUDRAH

CHAPTER 13

Riding up in the elevator, Noelle pondered Harmonie's problem. It had knocked Pamela's obnoxious behavior right out of her head, but the minute she stepped through the hotel suite door the other grandma was back in her windshield.

"Mom! Here you are! Pamela brought the children back an hour ago," Georgia called to her from the couch, where she sat with Kyle and the little ones.

Noelle hung up her coat and scarf, then walked over to join them. "Did they all have a nice time?"

"The Mouse King was the best!" Kenneth held a Nutcracker doll in his hands. For him, it was probably considered an 'action figure'.

"What did you like, Kelsey?"

"The Fairy," Kelsey had her eyes fixed on the cartoons on the TV screen. "And the little girl."

"Clara," Noelle said. "I think she's my favorite."

"You're certainly not Mother's favorite these days,"

Kyle said, not looking up from his laptop computer.

"Me? What do you mean, Kyle?" she asked.

He shook his head and wandered off toward the bar cart.

"What does he mean?" Noelle asked Georgia.

"Oh, Pamela just commented that you deciding to go to the Ballet threw her for a loop and put a shadow on the whole afternoon."

"Is that what the kids said, too?"

Georgia frowned. "No, of course not. Kids don't say things like that."

"They do, sometimes. If that's what they think."

"Well, they didn't say anything like that. But Pamela told Kyle she feels that you're crowding her."

"Kyle told you that?"

Georgia nodded.

"Well, it's only a few more days and I'll be gone from New York. And you'll go back to Cincinnati and everyone will be back on their own turf and in their own lane," Noelle said. "I'm starving, what's the plan for dinner?"

"Room service, Mom. We already ate," Georgia said.

"Yes, we all decided on a quiet evening in, after such a busy afternoon," Daisy said, as she and Trevor appeared in the living room.

"Is it dessert time, Nonny?" Kenneth asked.

Noelle put down the room service menu she'd been consulting and smiled at him. "Yes, of course, Kenneth. Cookies?"

If Noelle had planned the goodies in tonight's tin, she couldn't have put her finger on the pulse of anything better.

They were sandwich cookies, Isabel's specialty, in four different flavors. Vanilla, chocolate, orange, and coconut. At every cookie swap, every year, they were among the first to go and Noelle had headed straight for them, almost like a shopper finally let into the store after waiting all night before a Black Friday sale.

Tonight, she felt like the cream stuck in the middle of the sandwich, between her feelings for Matt and the reality of her family.

Kelsey and Kenneth had some competition for the cookies, now that Frost was in the picture. His little face lit up the moment he saw the cookie tin that she brought out for their 'refreshments' as they watched *The Polar Express*.

"Hitting a home run, there," Daisy said fondly, as she watched them. "Boy, do they need their Grandma."

Noelle knew they needed her. Loved her and wanted her around, maybe even all the time. But she was starting to realize that a better question was 'Did she need them? Only them?'

"By the way, Mom, where did the tree come from?"

Georgia looked up from the dining table where she was working on her laptop. "Mom's new friend, Matt, bought it for the kids."

Daisy looked impressed. "Decorations too?"

"Some of them," Noelle said. "Some of the hotel staff brought up a few things, too. The kids have been making friends, down in the lobby and among the chambermaids, and they all seemed to have a few extra things that they wanted to contribute to the Finch/Moran family tree."

"And we're going to have presents under it, too!"

Kenneth seemed to have one ear on their conversation, at the same time as he watched Santa's big bag of gifts hoisted onto the sleigh. "Matt says Santa knows where we are."

Georgia and Daisy looked at one another. "Yes, he does, dear,' Daisy said. "And is it all right if Uncle Trevor and I put our presents for you under the tree?"

Kenneth nodded so hard, it looked as though his head might take leave of his neck. "Yep. And Frost can put his stocking under the tree, too. Maybe we better go see Santa and tell him where Frost will be!"

"Oh, he knows, honey, he knows," Georgia said.

"So, what did you and Trevor and Kyle get up to today?" Noelle asked Daisy.

"We took him over to see Santa at the store and then for a walk in the park," Daisy said. "Then Trevor had a game he wanted to watch so we crashed at our hotel for a while, then came over here to see you."

Noelle smiled at her.

"We worked through the whole afternoon," Georgia said, coming back over to the couch with a giant bowl of popcorn that Kenneth and Kelsey claimed right away. "Had to get over to Tribeca for a tour of one of the stores and then back to West 56th for another meeting. The crowds and the traffic are just amazing. It's going to take some getting used to. Cincinnati is a city but it's nothing like this."

The silence went on so long that Noelle thought she could hear the ticking of a clock.

"What do you mean, 'getting used to'?" Daisy asked.

"You don't miss a beat, do you?" Georgia settled down in between her two youngsters and pulled a blanket over the three of them.

"Mom, what do you think she means?" Daisy was not going to stop with just a question as a response to her question.

"What's that, now?" Noelle barely heard half of the comments made around her now. Matt was on her mind every minute.

"The crowded sidewalks, Mom," Daisy said. "Georgia, why are you thinking about getting used to New York?"

Georgia rose, then settled Kenneth and Kelsey under the blanket. She laid a finger over her lips, then motioned Daisy and Noelle to follow her over to the other side of the living room.

"We haven't told the kids yet and I want to think about how to do that. We're moving to New York!" Her eyes were glittering and her face shouted excitement. "The company wants to extend our contract beyond the one year they gave us when they bought out our little shop in Cincinnati. They'll keep us on to work on other acquisitions and projects. Both Kyle and me! We'll be working with designers and very experienced marketing execs. And traveling! Places like Singapore and Paris!"

Daisy looked quite shocked. Noelle wasn't sure how she felt.

Her smile was tight. "Georgia, that's wonderful news."

"That's all you have to say, Mom?"

"Well, I'm very proud of you, dear. Of course."

Georgia crossed her arms. "What else, Mom?"

"That's all. I'll miss you, when you're living here in New York and doing all your international travel. I'm concerned that I won't see you as often."

"Oh Mom, of course, we'll still see you all the time! You get on an airplane, you go to visit somebody, what difference does it make whether it's Cincinnati or New York? I'm surprised, Mom, I thought you'd be really thrilled for me."

"I am, Georgia, I am."

She was pouting now. "Well, all right then. Thank you. There's more details but I won't bore you with them right now."

There are more details, Noelle thought.

"How soon does all this happen?" Daisy asked, to fill up the silence.

"Next month," Georgia said. "Right away."

"What about Kenneth and Kelsey?"

"Oh Mom. They have babysitters and housekeepers and nannies in New York, too. We'll be fine. They'll be fine."

Noelle had never felt so distant from her daughter. "I'm sure they will be. Well. This makes this Christmas week even more special. I'm so glad we're getting to spend all this time together."

Georgia smiled, and Noelle thought she picked up on some relief in her expression. "So am I, Mom, so am I. I'm glad you're getting so much time with them and they're so happy. They love New York!"

"I'm starting to see the attraction," Noelle said.

"It's a wonderful place and it will be a wonderful place for them to grow up," Georgia said. "You know, Mom, I really wish you'd reconsider about doing that TV feature with them, discovering the city."

Give her an inch and she wanted to go all the way across the Atlantic.

She locked on eye contact with Georgia. "Do you really? Does it really mean that much to you?"

Georgia nodded.

"Then, all right, maybe for a day. Or a half day," she said. Did Georgia have anybody else in her life who would do so much to shake her out of a pout? Maybe Kyle, although Noelle sometimes wondered whether Kyle noticed Georgia's moods much at all.

"I'll call Dan Keyes now," Georgia said, pulling out her cell phone.

Here we go.

**

When Matt walked through the hotel doors, he didn't expect to see a choir of Victoria carolers gathered around the giant Christmas tree, joyfully delivering their version of a Nat King Cole classic so loudly that Harmonie and her band were completely outdone.

He stood beside the fireplace and watched the dueling carols go one-on-one for a chorus or two. Harmonie caught his eye and they both grinned.

A few minutes later she gave up and signaled to the band to wrap up their tune. She watched the carolers for a minute, then joined in on their song, in their key. The drummer pitched in, then the keyboard player, and before long, the band and the carolers were united in what was turning into quite a concert. When *"The Christmas Song"* was finished, the acapella singers launched right into *"Jingle Bells"*. Harmonie and the band played along.

Donald, the concierge, was ready to pitch a fit. Matt saw him pick up the phone and shout at somebody at the other end of the line. He couldn't make out the words but he could tell they weren't festive.

A middle-aged, weary-looking man wearing a hotel jacket arrived at the elbows of the carolers in the tenor section. He waved at the choir director, as they wrapped up one song and plunged into the next. He tried waving, chopping the air, and drawing a finger across his throat, but he just couldn't get their attention. Or, maybe he did.

They were just wrapping up and passing the hat among an appreciative crowd of guests, when the police showed up.

"Excuse me, sir, excuse me, ma'am," the officer in the lead said as he cleared a path through the lobby. "Who's in charge here?"

"That would be me." Donald stepped forward.

"No, it wouldn't," said the middle-aged, exhausted man. "I'm the hotel manager, officer. But I'm not the one who called you."

'Who called us?"

"That would be me," the concierge repeated.

"Why?" The officer was looking at the crowd of happy guests, the Victorian carolers, and the jazz band.

"That was my question, too." The manager seemed to be getting taller while the concierge shrank.

Quite the show. Matt appreciated the distraction to pass the time while he thought about how he was going to speak to Noelle, now that he had followed his heart here. He had considered the idea of calling ahead to ask Noelle to meet him in the lobby but his suggestion that they get together after the ballet hadn't gone over so well and he wasn't eager to get shot down again.

He was hoping that now that she'd been back to the hotel, had heard the kids' comments about the show she'd wanted to be the one to take them to, and handed out her cookies or whatever, that she'd be more open to the idea of seeing him today.

He was very aware that she was only in town for a week. Of course, there were other women that he knew who would take his calls, but he wanted this one. He hadn't yet figured out why, exactly, but there was just something going on there. God help him, she was the only one he wanted to talk to.

He braced himself, then took out his phone.

Noelle?

I'm here.

I'm downstairs. Listening to Christmas carols and looking for someone to drown my sorrows with

What sorrows?

The hockey team just traded my favorite player

LOL. That's no sorrow.

Okay, how about to moisten my joys?

Blech. These metaphors are out of control

LOL. Come have a drink

All right. Ten minutes

He couldn't help it. He watched the elevator doors open and close during every one of the ten minutes he waited, setting himself up in the holly-green wingback chair right across from the spot where she would appear.

Numerous groups of holiday tourists came and went from their rooms. Most of them were smiling and chatting about something; those coming from the street brought with them a glow of fresh air and those coming from the restaurants or the shops brought the vibes of the well-fed or the otherwise satisfied. Oh, yeah, there were a few cranky ones, there always were—but they were a minority. It was the holidays, this was New York, and Matt couldn't think of any better place to be.

At long last, the elevator doors opened and there she was. Pretty, in a dark green dress, with her hair pinned up, this time. Matt jumped up and went to meet her.

"Thanks for coming downstairs," he said. I know I didn't give you much notice."

"You didn't give me any notice!" She was laughing, but her attention was distracted by the commotion going on the lobby, just over his shoulder. "Why are the police here?"

"It seems to be a case of trespassing singers—although our in-house musicians don't seem to mind. Maybe it's 'causing a holiday disturbance'?"

Noelle laughed. "Except that the holidays are nothing but disturbance, really."

"So, we don't know," Matt said.

She laughed again. "What are we going to do?"

"Do you want to go out? You didn't bring your coat. You're not really dressed for a winter walk."

"I know. I'd rather just stay here, maybe listen to Harmonie sing a few numbers. It'll be bath time for the kids soon."

So, he was on a timer again. Matt smothered his urge to comment as he led her toward the lobby bar. They both waved at Harmonie as they passed by; she was deep in conversation with one of the police officers.

"Matt, I have to thank you again for getting me that ticket to the ballet. It was absolutely one of my best times ever and I'll never forget it."

"You're very welcome," he said. "I only wish I could have seen it with you. But maybe we can do that another time."

He couldn't quite believe those words were coming out of his mouth. She didn't say anything, positive or negative, and the silence went on long enough to be awkward.

Once they were settled in front of the fireplace with drinks in hand, Matt said, "So, tomorrow is the day before Christmas Eve. What could we think of doing that would be fun?"

"Oh, no fun for me, I'm afraid. It's the big office Christmas party for Georgia and Kyle, the reason they came down to New York for this week in the first place. Everything has been building up to this event and they're . . . they're like they're on the edge of a ledge."

"Does this all have any impact on you, other than just knowing that's going on?"

"Oh, yeah. Big time. It's up to me to keep everything on an even keel, keep the little ones busy and happy, try to be Georgia's backup for anything she needs." She took another couple of sips of her wine. "And I've agreed to do the TV interview, with the grandkids."

"You have?" He wouldn't have been more surprised if she'd said she was going to take a weekend trip with a biker gang. "Why? I thought you really didn't want to waste any of your week on that sort of thing. And with that guy."

She looked at him with surprise, but decided to deal with the surface of the question and not its subtext.

"Because Georgia just seems kind of . . . fragile this week. And it seems to be very important to her, so I thought I'd say yes."

"Why is that up to you to fix, if she seems fragile? Wouldn't that be up to her husband?"

"Because I've been fixing things since she was a baby," Noelle said.

"Do you plan to stop, at any point?"

"Probably not."

"Does she fix things back for you?"

"No, she's there for her little ones. Paying it forward."

"So, who does, for you?"

He hadn't meant it as a rhetorical question, but it hung in the air like one. Something needed to happen to change the subject.

Noelle stared off across the lobby, where the police

officers were shaking hands with the Victorian carolers and making their way toward the door. Starting up her set again, Harmonie began a soulful rendition of *"The Twelve Days of Christmas"*.

"So, only three more sleeps," she said in a hearty voice that sounded completely fake.

"Yes, the big day is right around the corner," he said in an equally weird way. "Are you all ready? Did you ever find those robot toys you were hunting for?"

"I did not," Noelle said. "I've called toy stores all over town but no luck."

"You know, I think I saw in the Times that there is some kind of contest with one of those as a prize at Bry-ant Park tomorrow," he said. "A snow-man-building contest, I think."

"That might be fun for them. And maybe if I could win one, they could share it. Or I'd keep it as mine, and they'd have to come visit me, to play with it."

"Could I play with it, if I come to visit you?"

Again, the silence hung awkwardly. She seemed to be wrestling with herself.

"Yes, of course. I know you'd love to see the children figuring out a robot."

How much more obvious did he need to be? "Noelle, I couldn't care less about seeing your grandchildren. I wish you would care less about it."

"About what? About getting the mini GPT3s for them? Because that's been my main focus, after looking after Kenneth and Kelsey, for the past five days."

"I thought maybe I was becoming your focus. After Kenneth and Kelsey. Maybe before Kenneth and Kelsey."

Damn. He'd planned for it to go down in a much better way than this. Still, there was no turning back now.

Noelle stared at him. For a moment it looked as though she was leaning toward him, and he willed her in that direction with every ounce that he had.

"I barely know you," she said. "I only met you five days ago. I don't know where you grew up, where you went to school, what work you've done, what your marriage was like, how you get on with your kids. Nothing."

"So, let's talk. I'll answer all those questions. What it was like, working at the hospital. My friends, my hobbies. My favorite color, my childhood pets. I'll tell you about my kids, where they live, what they're like. But none of that is what's important."

"All I want is to get those special toys for them, Matt. That's all."

The words hung in the air, along with a whole lot more that weren't spoken. That's all. Not you. Not us. If you thought otherwise, you were mistaken. I don't have time for you, I'm not attracted to you, I don't want to get to know you better.

That's what he thought he heard, and it hurt. He stood up. "Thanks for joining me for a drink, Noelle."
And he was gone.

CHAPTER 14

When Noelle's phone rang Thursday morning and she saw Yvonne's name on the call display, she threw on her overcoat and stepped onto the balcony. It was cold, but it was private. Noelle had slept badly, and she still wasn't sure what had happened in her conversation with Matt last night. She needed Yvonne's opinion.

After she touched the video chat button, Isabel and Sherry's faces popped up, along with Yvonne's.

"Group chat!" Noelle said. "Fun!"

"I thought so," Yvonne said. "Sherry, how's the weather in the Caribbean? Make us jealous."

"It's fabulous, as you might have guessed." Sherry swung her phone around to show them the pool deck she was lounging on. "How are you all doing?"

"We're ready for Christmas!" Isabel said. "I have seventeen coming over tomorrow night, ten for dinner on Christmas Day."

"And you, Yvonne? Are you cooking?"

"I am. But only for four," she said. "How about you, Noelle? Probably not, I'm guessing, if you're at a hotel."

"You know, I don't really know what the plans are for Christmas dinner," Noelle said. "It's been chaotic here, to say the least. Georgia is so wrapped up in work and I haven't really felt like it's my place to take over and start planning. So, I just hang back and try to go with the flow."

"How are you, kid?" Yvonne asked. "You sound a bit low."

"Oh, I think I'm just still a bit off balance. Not my usual routines and all that. You know."

"How's that nice man you met?" Sherry asked. "I think he's gone."

"What? Already? It's only been a few days!" They all spoke at once.

"What new man?" Isabel asked. "I only talked to you a day or so ago, and you didn't say anything about meeting a man."

"Well, we were focusing on you," Noelle said. "And Rob. How are things going?"

Even on the small phone screen, she could see Isabel make a face. "Pretty much the same. But we have a lot to do with the holidays, so that's keeping the focus off us."

"Back to the new man, Noelle," Sherry said impatiently. "Did he not like your family? Is that it? You should have held off on introducing him to the whole crowd."

"No, I don't think that was it," Noelle said. "It was me, not them."

"Was it him, too?" Sherry was following her investigating instincts.

"Yeah, I think so," Noelle said. "I think it was both of us."

The buzz was definitely killed, and the four of them sat in silence for a few moments. "Well, that's a shame," Yvonne finally said. "I think it sounded like he was someone you could like."

"I don't know what I like, Yvonne!" Why did it feel to Noelle as if that were some sort of explosion?

"I don't really know what I like or what I want. I can't remember who I was or what I liked before Ian. Even, all those years in the classroom, I was always thinking about my students, what they needed. So, it's just as well that my kids and my grandkids take up so much of my time."

"You wouldn't know what to do with your time otherwise?" Sherry asked. "Honey, I'd show you."

They all laughed.

"Yeah, Sherry, what about a new man for you, down there in the tropics?" Yvonne asked.

Noelle was happy to feel the spotlight move away.

When they rang off, a few minutes later, after agreeing to connect again soon, Noelle stood on the balcony for a while longer. She was still thinking about Matt and she couldn't seem to get her mind to go in any other direction. She picked up her phone and called his number.

Straight to voice mail.

She didn't leave a message; she had no idea what to say. But he would see that she had phoned, that she was thinking of him, and he could call her back. His turn to take a leap.

Throughout the rest of the early morning, while the little ones had breakfast and Georgia and Kyle fussed about their big office Christmas party coming up that evening, Noelle listened for the buzz of her phone. She checked it about a dozen times, just in case a call had come in with no sound an-nouncing it; that had been known to happen.

Nothing.

She still didn't know why he was being like this. Of course, her thoughts had gone straight to her usual style of blaming herself: she must have said something that put him off or upset him. She did allow the other voice in her head to suggest for a few moments that perhaps it had something to do only with him, and that perhaps there was nothing to blame herself for, but it didn't take long for the clouds and the guilt to roll in.

Noelle could hear the kids inside, arguing with their dad over what breakfast they would eat.

"Who would like to come out with me to look at the toys in the store windows?" She tried to make it sound like more fun than they'd ever had. They were a bit suspicious at first but after a few minutes her relentless cheeriness won them over and they started galloping around the living room, chanting "the store windows! the store windows!"

"And . . . I heard about a snowman-building contest that we could go see!"

"Yeah, snowmen!"

Two for two.

"And maybe a tour of movie locations! Places in New York where they did famous movies like *Elf* and *Home Alone*!"

The two little ones looked at her with blank faces. Okay, two out of three. Still, not bad.

She decided to start with the snowman-building contest

at Bryant Park. Somehow, she wanted to be in a place where she'd once been with him.

As soon as Noelle saw the skaters gliding across the ice, every second of their hours there earlier in the week came back to her. She spotted a man with silver hair and a black topcoat in the lineup at the roasted chestnuts cart ahead of them and she thought for a breathless moment that coincidence had brought him to this exact same place at the same time this morning.

Her heart sank when she saw a tall woman in a dark blue coat and silver boots reach over and tuck her hand behind his arm. So that was it. That must have been the reason he had seemed so cold toward her yesterday, and wouldn't return her texts or phone calls. He'd met somebody new—or he'd been with somebody, all along. Noelle barely knew the man and yet when she thought of him with somebody else, she felt sick to her stomach.

Then, he turned around. Not the same man.

So, here she was, two days before the big holiday. Freezing cold, getting rattled by imaginary Matts, still not ready for Christmas morning . . . and she didn't even like roasted chestnuts.

But Noelle was determined to find at least one bright spot in this day. In fact, once she got her chin up and took a look around, she could find dozens.

A miniature train had been added to the festivities. Bryant Park was full of families, the children running around, their parents smiling, all of them playing in the snow. Various snow men and snow women were in various stages of construction; Kenneth and Kelsey were eager to get started on theirs.

Noelle helped them turn their first snowball into a snowman bottom that was big enough, then walked a few feet over to the event table, which was decorated with signs proclaiming it a fund-raising event for the library and asking for donations.

One other sign caught Noelle's eye. This was a fund-raising event, it was a family fun event, and it was also a possible source of a mini GPT3 robot. The creator of the winning snow person en-ry would take home the prize.

Noelle turned back to Kenneth and Kelsey, pitching in to help lift the snowman's tummy into place.

"What are you planning to do for eyes, a nose, and a mouth?"

She knew that voice. "Hello, Pamela. What brings you here?"

"Georgia told me this was in the grandkids' schedule for today," Pamela said.

"Hi, Grandma!" Kenneth called to her over his shoulder as he continued to sculpt the snowman's bottom two parts. "We're building."

"I see that," Pamela said. "Very nice."

"And after this, we're going to see windows!" Kelsey announced.

"Windows?"

"Department store windows," Noelle said. "To look at the toys. Maybe do some shopping."

"Aren't you ready yet? I've got mine all set. Had some last-minute good luck."

"Well, good for you," Noelle said. "Excuse me." She walked around Pamela to hand Kenneth a handful of stones to add to the snowman's column of buttons.

"You know, Noelle, I have to apologize for my comments yesterday at the ballet."

Whoa, now. This was unexpected.

"I've talked with Georgia and I realize now that you have no interest in someone like Matt as a date, or a special friend. Or in anybody, for that matter. Your interest is the wellbeing of your grandchildren. As is mine . . . although I might have a little more time available than you. And resources. . . . ever since Connor and I split up, I've been able to make ends meet on my own."

Noelle glanced at Pamela's coat and boots. She did more than just make ends meet.

"And New York is my town, Noelle. I love it that you're here to visit for a week, and I hope you get around to liking the place a little bit. But surely you can see that one New Yorker is going to have more in common with another than with an out-of-towner."

Noelle brushed her gloved hands together, sweeping snow down to the ground. "Pamela, Matt and I are not an item in any way. He gave me the ballet ticket because he knows that I love the Nutcracker and he wanted me to see how good the New York performance is. I have no interest in having a date or a 'special friend', as you call it. I'm a grandma, and family is everything."

"Yes, of course it is," Pamela said. She was no stranger to sarcasm.

They stared at each other and Noelle imagined she could read the other grandmother's mind. *You need to act your age, Noelle. Women like you shouldn't chase after unattainable men.*

The silence was broken by a man's voice. "Well, look who it is!"

Noelle turned around. "Hello, Mr. Keyes," she said. "Let me guess. My daughter told you where we'd be."

"That's half the story," Dan said. "I have an appointment to meet with her and your son-in-law at their office at noon. I'm over here first to get some great action footage of the kids making snowmen with their grandma and trying to win a very special toy."

"You won't let me get out of this TV report, will you?" Noelle didn't know why, but suddenly she felt wearier than she had in years. Excuse me, the kids are calling."

They weren't, but Noelle whooped at Kenneth, scooped Kelsey up into a hug, and led them on a run, threading her way in between and around all the snowmen and snow families.

"Come on, let's have a ride!" she said as she lifted them on board the Christmas train. They sat on the wooden benches and rode through the market, the Candy Cane Lane, and among the trees decorated with dreidels.

When they got back to the center of the park, Pamela and Dan Keyes were gone and the organizers were just about to announce the winner of the miniGPT3 robot. Noelle held her breath as the man pulled a piece of paper from the entry box and unfolded it.

"Ricardo Juarez!" He announced, and Noelle heard a whoop of joy from somewhere back in the crowd. Ricardo Juarez wins the robot toy and she was unlucky again. How many times was that?

She shook off her disappointment. They took a taxi over to one of the main shopping streets and spent a wonderful hour gazing through the glass at the sparkling, dazzling displays of technical and toy-making wizardry in the stores' windows.

Kenneth and Kelsey's cheeks were like rosy apples, their hair and eyelashes tinged with ice by the time another taxi dropped them back at the hotel. Noelle hustled them through the cozy lobby, stopping to stare at the giant Christmas tree.

"Are we making a wish, Nonny?" Kelsey asked.

"What?"

"Teacher says to make a wish on the star at the top of a Christmas tree."

"Maybe we are, Kelsey, maybe we are making a wish," Noelle said.

Inside the hotel suite, Georgia and Kyle were locked in party preparation. This company holiday event had been planned for six months, Georgia told her, and it was the main reason they were in New York. Georgia swept into the room in her party dress just as Noelle was setting the table with sugar cookies covered in red and green icing.

"Georgia! You look beautiful! What a dress," Noelle said as she sat Kelsey on a cushion and pulled her chair up to the table.

"You think so, Mom? Thank you!" Georgia did a little twirl, her stiletto heels tapping on the hardwood floor.

"I do think so. Wow," she said, stopping to give her daughter her full attention.

The dress was a deep midnight blue, with silver sparkles very subtly scattered along the neckline. It was quite covered up in the front but the back was cut lower, to a tight fit around her ribcage, then draping in an expensive way over

Georgia's hips.

"I'm so nervous," Georgia said, carefully sitting down on the edge of a chair across the table from the kids. "You guys stay over there on your side, okay? I don't want to get any cookie crumbs on this dress. By the way, Mom, that's quite a cookie! Look at all that icing. Are you sure they should be having so much sugar this time of night?"

"Don't worry about it, dear," Noelle said. "I'm the one who will cope with it, if they get all sugared up. But somehow, I don't think they will." Both kids' little heads seemed to be dropping already; all the fresh air and exercise of the day had worked their magic.

"Oh, I forgot to mention to you, Mom," Georgia said. "Pamela is going to drop by for a few minutes tonight. And Daisy and Trevor are coming over, too."

"The party is here," Noelle commented.

"Don't worry, they'll all be gone by eight."

"Why is Pamela coming over?"

"She wants to talk to drop off gifts."

"The robot toys?"

"No, none of us has found them."

"I entered a snowman-building contest today, trying to win one," Noelle said.

"I know, Kenneth told me. He said he wasn't disappointed at all, although he did think his snowman was the best, and should have won. But he says Santa will be bringing him one, anyway."

Noelle shook her head. "Santa is a wonderful idea, but it's not an easy idea, sometimes. You do what you can to create the magic, but it's not easy."

"I get that," Georgia said. "I never did before I had kids, but I do now."

"There's a lot of things you find out after you actually have kids," Noelle said. "You have a lot of opinions beforehand, but then you find out the reality."

They both laughed just as the suite doorbell was ringing. Georgia went to answer it, then returned with Daisy, Trevor, and Frost. Daisy headed straight for the wine glasses.

"What a day we've had! Do you have any idea what it's like to be out with little kids in New York City? Oh, of course you do. Well, anyway, we tried MOMA, we tried the Met, we tried Fifth Avenue, we tried Central Park—nothing worked for him. Finally, we just decided to go back to the hotel and crash. But then, just getting over here, we had about twelve emergencies. I'm telling you, Mom, it would have been so much easier to do Christmas at home in Portland."

Noelle took an open bottle of white wine out of the refrigerator and poured a glassful for Daisy. "Relax, dear, it's all over now. You're here. Let Trevor entertain the kids for a while." She looked over at the table. "Looks like he's found the cookie tin and a chair for him and Frost. Speaking of daddies, where's Kyle?"

"Still getting ready to go to the holiday party," Georgia said. "He's totally stressed. It's going to be a big night."

Kenneth and Kelsey had wandered over to their toy stash and were getting into a complicated game of action figure soldier rescuing princess.

"I guess the cartoons finally got boring," Georgia said. "Let's put on the news for a few minutes while they're busy."

She pointed the remote at the screen.

"Look, there's that TV reporter who was here. Dan Keyes. The one who wanted to hang out with Mom."

"Really." Daisy raised an eyebrow. 'Kinda creepy, isn't it?"

"Creepy for a man to want to spend time with me?" Noelle asked.

"No, I didn't mean that." Daisy scrambled. "I meant creepy to use your job as a way to try to meet women."

"I don't think that's what he was doing, Daisy," Noelle said. "He was genuinely interested in showing the story of the families that flock to New York over the holidays and he wanted to have us as his example. That's all."

Neither Daisy nor Georgia looked convinced. "Well, all right. If you say so, Mom."

Georgia snapped off the TV. "It's too bad you didn't want to let him put you and the kids on TV, but I am glad he didn't turn out to want to date you. Unlike that other guy."

"Matt?" Georgia looked back and forth between Georgia and Daisy. "What's wrong with Matt?"

"It's not him in particular, Mom, it's anybody," Daisy said.

"What do you mean?"

Daisy said nothing, just shook her head.

"Thanks for leaving me to do the heavy lifting, Daisy," Georgia said. "Look. Mom. It's a bit silly for people to carry on like teenagers when they're your age. We've got nothing against Matt. Maybe he's a nice man. But you're fifty-five, for Heaven's sake!"

"And nobody can replace Dad," Daisy spoke very softly, but Noelle heard every word.

"Oh, Daisy, no one will replace your dad. He was a unique individual, and no one replaces another. He was your dad, the only one you had, and nothing will ever change that."

In all the years with Ian, she had never discussed the truth about her marriage with them, and now that he was gone, she doubted she ever would.

Noelle pulled each of them with one arm into a hug. "And don't worry. Matt is no longer in the picture."

"Why? What happened?" Georgia asked.

Noelle waved off the question. "Doesn't matter. He's gone."

"Are you upset about it?"

"It's Christmas!" Noelle said. "I don't plan to be upset about anything."

Half an hour later, Daisy lifted a sleeping Frost from the couch and carried him off to the rest of the night back at her and Trevor's hotel. Georgia and Kyle hustled out of the door in a blaze of Christmas finery with goodnight kisses for Kenneth and Kelsey.

They could barely keep their eyes open and just moments after their parents left, they were fast asleep. Noelle picked up Kelsey, enjoying the coziness of her warm, heavy, sleeping little body in red flannel pajamas. She didn't stir as Noelle carried her down the hallway to the bed.

When she returned to the living room, Kenneth appeared to have gone even deeper into sleep. It was a challenge, but she managed to pick him up, too, and moments later had him tucked into his bed.

Noelle flopped down on the couch. Man, she was ready for some peace and quiet. She was used to being alone most of the time and this week of non-stop companionship had taken some getting used to.

She found the remote where Georgia had dropped it and turned on the TV, surfing through a tidal wave of holiday movies and department store commercials.

Her phone buzzed, and she almost ignored it. She really didn't want to talk to anybody or think about anything for a while.

But it might be Georgia or Daisy and there might be something she was needed for.

She picked up the phone.

I'm downstairs in the lobby and I want to come up, just for a few minutes.

Wha-a-at?

Noelle picked up her reading glasses so that she could take a good look at the call display.

Pamela Finch. The last person she wanted to see this evening. She'd forgotten that Georgia had told her Pamela was stopping by.

Noelle typed her reply as quickly as she could, trying to head her off at the pass.

The kids are already asleep.

There was a delay, and Noelle thought she could feel Pamela's irritation vibing up through the phone.

It will only take a minute. They can go right back to sleep after

I leave. I want to give them their gifts so they can see them under the tree.

Tomorrow would work.

I don't know if I'll be able to get over this way tomorrow, Noelle.

I don't know if I'll be able to wake them up.

Try.

Why don't you just bring the gifts up and I'll put them under the tree for you.

Because I want to see the kids. Why did you put them to bed so early?

Had no choice. They fell asleep.

Noelle glanced at the TV at a scene from a movie about finding an elusive Christmas gift. She waited.

Why are you so determined to keep me away from my grandchildren?

Whoa.

I am not doing any such thing. This is too heavy to be discussing over text.

We've got issues we need to sort out.

But not over text. And I can't invite you here now. I'm just exhausted.

I don't want to talk to you either.

Some other time?

Don't bother.

CHAPTER 15

Noelle expected the morning to begin in a leisurely way, after such a late night for Georgia and Kyle at the Christmas party.

When she wandered into the suite's living room at seven o'clock, she thought she'd have the space to herself for a while, but Georgia was already there, sipping a cup of coffee and scrolling through the latest on her phone.

"Good morning, Mom!" she said. "How was your night?"

"Just fine, dear." Well, that wasn't entirely true. But how do you tell your thirty-year-old daughter that you were awake for three-quarters of the night, missing a man you barely knew and freezing because he wasn't there to warm you up? "How was your party?"

"Went well, I think. Met some new people, people we'll be working with a lot. Got introduced to everybody."

Noelle brought the coffeepot over and offered to refresh Georgia's cup. "Why are you up and dressed so early?"

"On our way in half an hour. Meetings. Thanks, Mom." Georgia barely looked up from the phone screen.

Noelle sat down. "On Christmas Eve?"

"Yes, on Christmas Eve. Mom, not everybody is retired like you. I have things I have to get done today."

Noelle counted to ten. "You're right, not everyone is retired like me. But lots of people like you manage busy lives and have very responsible jobs and also make time for their children."

"I make time for my children!" That pulled Georgia's attention away from her phone screen. But should it be necessary to shock or insult her in order to get a response?

"I thought you might come along with us to visit the hotel kitchen," Noelle said. "Chef Justin offered a special tour, just for the kids, before this Grand Buffet we're all going to."

"Oh, yeah, that's on around eleven, isn't it? Do you have the tickets or do I have the tickets? Maybe Kyle has the tickets. But no, Mom, sorry. We can't stay home all day. But I'm going to compress eight or ten hours or work into three so that I can be there for the Buffet."

"It's Christmas Eve, sweetheart. They're four years old and six years old. They'll be twelve before you know it, and then they'll want to be with their friends. Cherish these years and give them as much time as you can. And then double or triple that, and give them more."

Georgia looked as weary and deflated as only an overworked parent can. "Mom, I'd love to, but my job is just so intense. You have no idea. Being an executive vice-president at an international company has you going 24/7."

"I know, dear, I know. Or I can try to imagine. And I'm not suggesting you quit your job or dial back on your career."

Noelle wished for a car ride, a place they needed to go together, so that they could sit side by side and have a difficult conversation, like they'd done when Georgia was a teenager.

She cleared her throat. "Georgia, I have to say—international companies have hundreds of vice-presidents. They come and they go. I hope this isn't offensive or disrespectful to say, but the world won't notice, thirty years from now, that you were a vice-president."

"Executive vice-president."

"Executive vice-president. The world has lots of those. Kenneth and Kelsey only have one mom and one dad. It only makes sense to work this way if it makes you happy. And if it's the right thing for your family."

"But we have to make a living, Mom!"

"Only you can know how much of a living you need to make, sweetie. It's all about balance. You make your choices."

Kyle called from the bedroom. "Georgia!" His voice sounded quite distressed.

"I have to go see what's going on," Georgia said.

Noelle wasn't alone very long before Kenneth arrived, his eyes still sleepy.

"I'm hungry, Nonny," he said, climbing into her lap. He was growing so big; he wouldn't fit much longer.

"What would you like for breakfast?" she asked.

"My cereal," he said, and she went off to fill a bowl for him.

"Mom, we're going!" Georgia's voice called from the hallway. "We'll be back by eleven, for the Buffet!"

"See you then!" Noelle called, but her words came out seconds after she heard the door close.

**

When Noelle had offered to drop by to help Chef Justin get ready for the Christmas Eve Buffet, she thought it would be fun for the kiddies to see a professional kitchen in action.

The subject came up a few days later and Pamela butted right in. She had become an expert at that, where her grandchildren were concerned.

She raised half a dozen safety concerns: what if someone dropped a hot liquid on them? What if something were spilled, the floor was not cleaned properly, and one of the children slipped? Who are all these people who will be in the kitchen? Have they all had background checks?

Noelle had soothed Georgia's concerns, ignored Pamela's, and gone ahead with her plans to accept Chef Justin's invitation.

Before the visit to the hotel kitchen, Noelle wanted to try to come up with a mini-GPT3 robot. One more time! If she could only find even one, maybe the kids could be persuaded to share, then Daisy and Georgia could pass it around, send it from city to city?

She searched out the top five toy stores in New York and called the first one.

"Hey, good morning. I'm looking for—"

No dice.

She worked through the rest of her list:

"Yes, of course, Happy Holidays to you too. I'm looking for a mini-GPT3 robot—"

"Yes, I know it's the top toy this Christmas, but I thought—"

"Yes, I'm sure you're busy, but—"

"Is there any chance somebody returned one? Changed their mind? Or maybe—"

"Okay, you don't have to laugh, just say—"

Noelle looked at the phone in her hand. Well, that was helpful.

"Nonny! Is it time to go to see the cooks?"

And in that moment, Noelle gave up. Yes, it was time to go see the cooks.

In the elevator, Kenneth and Kelsey were so excited that they couldn't stop talking and asking questions. Would they get to eat everything? Should they wash their hands first? What kind of food would it be? Why were they cooking now when the lunch wasn't until lunch? What was a buffet, anyway? Why was Santa coming? Would he have lunch? If he didn't stay for lunch, could they talk to him, anyway?

Noelle listened to them, but she didn't hear them. Matt was on her mind nonstop again; really, when would this end? She hadn't had an experience like this since before she was married, and maybe not even then.

She got it, she'd fallen hard for the man, but it just hadn't worked out. Whatever it was that she had said or done, he was gone, clearly. She'd tried texting him, phoning him, and sending him messages through the atmosphere. As if that ever worked. He just wasn't responding and wasn't open to her anymore. Not interested.

"Do you think they'll let me lick the spoon?" Kelsey wanted to know.

Noelle brought herself back to earth. "I'm sure if there are any spoons to lick, your pal Chef Justin will make sure you're in the lineup to get one," she said.

The elevator doors opened. "Inside voices, kids. Keep your hands near yourself, and be nice to everybody," Noelle said. "Come on."

They walked through the main restaurant toward the swinging doors that led to the kitchen.

Justin and Harmonie were standing at the back, smiling, and waiting to greet them. They squatted down to be on eye level for a few minutes with the kids—something a lot of young, non-parents don't think to do—then straightened up and led the way in. Harmonie, in her tight, sequined stage dress, looked as though she was relieved to stand up again.

The kitchen was the size of two of the classrooms Noelle remembered teaching in. Stainless steel ovens and stovetops stretched out in both directions, with refrigerators and sinks also dotting the landscape. She'd seen professional kitchens in movies and on TV shows, but like so many other recreations, it was just not quite like the real thing.

A dozen chefs and sous-chefs in white jackets zipped back and forth through the kitchen, between the long lines of stainless-steel ovens and stove tops, never once getting in one another's way.

The Dickens Christmas Eve Buffet was the highlight of the year for the Atlas March Royal Hotel, and everyone was at the top of their game. Chef Justin roamed around the kitchen, supervising the work of the others, who all bent over their dishes, taking meticulous care with every step and every detail of the food they were preparing.

And oh, the food they were preparing! The aromas were intoxicating: stuffed pork tenderloin; pepper-crusted beef tenderloin with mushrooms; Yorkshire pudding; turkey with all the fixings; shrimp and crab casserole; Coquilles Saint-Jacques; Louisiana Jambalaya; Lasagna Bolognese, manicotti, ravioli. Noelle stared at vegetable dishes by the dozen: braised kale, sautéed Brussels sprouts; scalloped potatoes; perfect mashed potatoes; candied yams; roasted asparagus; maple bacon carrots; green bean casserole; stuffed mushrooms; ricotta puffs; mushroom empanadas.

Appetizers took up one whole section of the kitchen, with trays on wheeled carts ready to go: pastry wreaths dotted with olives and peppers; turkey sliders with ginger and horse-radish; baked new potatoes with mozzarella and pesto; bruschetta with blue cheese and onion jam—Noelle was almost as overwhelmed as the kids were by everything there was to see.

One large, empty table had a taped label: Breads. Noelle could just imagine the cheddar and sourdough biscuits, pesto breadstick twists, pillowy dinner rolls, and focaccia that would make their appearances there when it was time to go out up to the main ballroom on the mezzanine, where the Charles Dickens Buffet would start very soon.

The pastry and dessert station was perhaps the busiest of all, with plum pudding, trifle, yule log cake, pound cake, bread pudding, red velvet cake, tiramisu, New York cheesecake, and cakes decorated to look like ugly Christmas sweaters, presented alongside plates heaping with a dozen kinds of Christmas cookies.

She knew that the dessert table would be the one that would dazzle most of the crowd but for her, it was the table next to it, where a cheese course was laid out in an array of dishes and plates unlike any she'd ever seen. Slices of every cheese she'd ever heard of and quite a few she hadn't were displayed on bone china with tiny touches of holly hand-painted on gold rims. She looked around to make sure no one was watching her, then pinched a slice of gruyere and popped it into her mouth. Oh. Heavenly.

She strolled back to a spot near the turkeys where Justin and Harmonie stood, watching the little ones.

"I think they like it," Justin whispered to Noelle and Harmonie, nodding toward Kenneth and Kelsey, whose eyes were as big as the plates stacked up to be taken up to the ball-room and set out at the ends of the buffet tables.

"Are you kidding? They're in heaven," Noelle said. "Thanks so much for inviting us down here to see this. It will be easy now to get them into their holiday clothes, when they know they're coming to eat here."

"What did you think of it?" Harmonie asked.

"Fabulous, just fabulous!" Noelle said. "I've never seen so much food all in one place. And it looks just wonderful. I can't wait till it's time for our seating."

"What looks the best to you?" Justin asked.

"Well, it's hard to say what will be the best, before I've tasted anything you've cooked, but just on display—and based on what I like best, which is savory rather than sweet—I'd have to say that cheese table is the best."

"You like cheeses?" Harmonie asked.

"My absolute favorite food," Noelle said.

"Make sure you stop by the ball-room on your way back up to see the décor before the crowds come in," Justin suggested. "And let's call Kenneth and Kelsey over here. I've got a little gift to send them off."

Even after the kids had seen all that premium holiday feast food, they seemed to be even more thrilled with Justin's gift of candy canes. After thanking him, they followed their grandma up the escalator, past the gigantic tree in the lobby, to the mezzanine, and off to the ballroom.

Harmonie had come along to take a peek with them. "Look, there's a throne over there!" she said. "Santa will sit there when he gets here."

The décor was stunning. After decades of silver, bronze, gold, and platinum dominating the holiday festive look everywhere, red and green were back. Giant ornaments covered the super-sized trees dotted throughout the ball-room. Noelle spotted a majestic chair in a corner and nudged Kelsey. Santa was coming!

And right beside Santa's throne, up on a little pedes-tal, there was a mini-GPT3 robot toy.

"Harmonie! I've been looking for that toy all over town!"

Harmonie gazed around the ballroom, in the final phases of preparation for the public, and waved at a tiny man in jockey silks and a straw fedora. "That's Dawson, the hotel decorator. We'll ask him about it."

"Oh yes, darling, we've had that for weeks. Seemed the right touch of futuristic thing contrasting with the an-cient history of Santa, am I right?"

"Is there any chance I could buy it after the Buffet is over?" Noelle murmured, watching the kids as they went over to inspect Santa's throne .

"No, it'll be in place tomorrow, during both Christmas Dinner seatings," Dawson said.

"What about after that?" She could always give it to the kids as a Merry "next day" gift.

"It's spoken for, after that," Dawson said.

Noelle nodded. She wasn't surprised. "Thanks, anyway. Thank you, Harmonie. I'm looking forward to hearing you sing. Soon, I guess. I'd better get these guys upstairs to get dressed for the party."

When they got back to the suite, the kids carried their candy canes off to the couch and put on the *Grinch*. Noelle had about an hour until the time stated on their Buffet tickets and they would have their turn to go down to eat. She figured she'd need that much and more to pull something together to wear.

One part of her wanted just to hang out upstairs in a pair of old sweats and give the whole thing a pass. Another part felt defiant and ready to break out. The second part won the argument, and she pulled out the dress that Harmonie had loaned her. It was elegant and very New York, but she wanted to liven it up. After all, it was Christmas Eve!

She went into Georgia's closet. A gorgeous red velvet jacket caught her eye; the size was perfect. A glittering silver belt changed the look of the dress—and there were heels to match!

They were a lot more heels than she could usually manage, but she didn't plan to walk far. Just down to the hotel ballroom and over to a chair near the Buffet. Worth a little sore-feet time—they really were so pretty.

The suite's doorbell rang and when Noelle opened it, Pamela was standing there. Oh, great.

"I brought the kids' Christmas gifts over to put under

the tree. Is anybody else here?" she said.

"I'm here," Noelle said. "Georgia and Kyle are at work."

She swore she could feel Pamela's foot tapping on the hardwood floor. "May I come in?"

After their text exchange last night? Noelle decided she'd had it, and it was time for transparency, as they called it nowadays. "Why should I invite you in, after you were so rude to me last night?"

"Me rude to you?! You were the bitchy one."

"I didn't use that word, Pamela. We're too busy to see you right now." Noelle continued to stand in the doorway.

Pamela looked as though she might explode. "Noelle, we have to sort this out. Georgia and Kyle are going to be moving to New York. The grandkids will be here. I'll be able to see them often. I don't want you to feel like we have edged you out."

Why would what Pamela wanted her to feel have anything to do with anything?

Noelle felt some other thought nagging at the edges of her mind, but she brushed it aside. "That's a much longer conversation than I want to have, standing in a doorway," she said.

"Not in a doorway, not on text last night. When would it be a good time for Her Majesty?"

"Now, that's not fair," Noelle said. "You say you want to talk things over, but then you throw in crap like that."

The two women locked eyes, and would have stayed there, tied up in a standoff until evening, if Noelle hadn't heard her phone ringing in the living room.

She walked away from the door and went to her phone. Georgia's name was on the call display.

"Hi, sweetie, what's up?"

"Mom, I'm so sorry, but we can't get away. We're doing the final decisions and announcements about staffing for the New Year and we have to get it done before we break for the rest of the holidays. You understand. . . "

Georgia was waiting for her to say something, but she just couldn't.

"Mom, we want to tell them the good news if they're promoted and not leave them hanging on, over Christmas, if they're not. You understand." Georgia paused again to give Noelle a chance to say something.

All she could think of was "Get your little butt home here, right now, or you'll be in big trouble, missy." Ha. Of course, that would be the wrong thing to say. Big time.

"Mom?"

Noelle took a deep breath. "So, you won't be coming to the Charles Dickens Christmas Buffet?"

"No, we can't be back in time for that. But we'll be there for dinner, and carols, and stuffing stockings after the kids go to bed."

"Okay, sweetie, see you then." Noelle cut off the call before Georgia could hear the catch in her voice.

Why was she letting this matter so much?

Noelle looked over at the door of the suite. Pamela was still standing there, looking down at her shoes. Noelle wasn't sure whether or not she was surprised to see her there, but she was startled to see a soft smile on Pamela's face when she looked up.

"Noelle, I'm sorry. You're right, it was crap. I guess I just have one method for trying to get my way, and that's elbows out, walking fast. It's the New York way," she said. "Really, I mean it, we need to find a way to coexist here."

Noelle stared at her for a moment. "So, I have an extra ticket or two for this Christmas buffet lunch," she said. "Do you want to come along with us?"

If Pamela was relieved, she didn't show it. "That would be lovely."

Noelle stood aside and Pamela stepped into the room. "Kenneth, Kelsey. Grandma's here."

**

The mood in the ballroom had changed during the hour since Noelle had been there last. Almost every seat was taken now by adults and children in their holiday finery, and the banquet tables were covered in snowy white linen, overlaid with platter after platter of the food that Noelle had seen in the kitchen.

A jolly, well-groomed Santa in a very nice red velvet suit held court from his throne.

Pamela and Noelle guided the little kids up and down the rows of tables, helping them to manage their plates. Noelle pointed out Harmonie to them and they all enjoyed the beautiful sounds she and her band spread out over the room. She spotted the hotel manager and the concierge, nodding their heads in time to the music and smiling at Harmonie. Thank goodness that storm seemed to have blown over.

Noelle had had many wonderful Christmas celebrations at home in Vermont, but she'd never seen anything like this, and she had to admit that New York continued to amaze her. She wished Matt was around, so that she could tell him so.

She was thrilled to see, though, that Harmonie and Justin seemed to be doing alright. She watched him come over to her at the end of her set and help her down, on her towering heels, from the stage set up at the windows end of the room.

They found their way over to their seats. Even Trevor looked happy to be there. Noelle carried Kelsey's loaded plate in her other hand, Pamela carried Kenneth's, and Daisy brought up the rear with Frost. Knives and forks in hand, for the next few minutes, everyone had nothing to say.

"You seem to be enjoying yourself, Pamela," Noelle said, leaning toward her and speaking quietly.

"I am. It's an amazing event," Pamela said. "It really is. But I am a little disappointed that Georgia and Kyle didn't make it back in time."

"I'm a lot disappointed," Noelle said.

"We only get a limited number of Christmas Eves," Pamela said.

Noelle looked at her, really seeing her, and they nodded at one another.

It wasn't much, but it was a start.

Once they'd finished eating, servers appeared to clear their plates and go from table to table with coffee and tea for the adults, plus candy canes for all the children. Noelle felt like she'd eaten enough food to last for three days.

"Come on, we need some exercise," she said to Kenneth and Kelsey. "Let's get out for a walk."

"We'll come along with you," Daisy said.

When they emerged from the hotel, a light snow had started. It wasn't cold, though. The six of them strolled along, looking in windows, watching the people, and chatting. Noelle noticed a magnificent building behind an ornate wrought-iron fence.

"What's that, I wonder?"

Daisy stooped to read a plaque mounted by the front gate. "St. Mary's," she said. "Looks like there's a service start-ing

DEVIN AUDRAH

CHAPTER 16

They climbed the broad marble steps toward the triple wooden doors. A few dozen people in front of them were going in, and each time the doors opened Noelle could hear the sound of voices, soprano through to bass, joined in a celebration of the season.

"Let's see what's inside," she said.

She got no pushback, and Kenneth and Kelsey looked quite intrigued. Daisy and Trevor seemed content to slide into a pew and sit in silence, gazing up at the stained-glass windows, the marble pillars, and the gold-leaf details on the statues.

After two carols, the minister came forward and began readings from the Bible.

Noelle's phone lit up with a text and she looked around, almost feeling afraid that she might be smote for daring to bring technology into the house of the Lord.

We wrapped up early. Back at the hotel. Where are you?

Noelle almost snorted. Georgia thought this was early? She considered not answering, but then decided to relent.

St. Mary's Church

Noelle listened to the choir singing and felt the most peace she'd found in days.

We're going to come over to join you

Noelle smiled as she whispered to Kenneth. "Mommy's coming. And Daddy."

Georgia and Kyle arrived at the church about ten minutes before the service ended, just in time to sing "*O Holy Night*" and "*Joy to the World*" with their family.

They walked out into the late afternoon, blinking like little underground creatures suddenly released into the sunlight. The air was gentle and the snowfall soft. It was magical.

"Let's walk back to the hotel," Noelle said to Georgia as she watched Kyle raise his arm to call a taxi.

"I think Kyle wants to get back," Georgia said.

"I'll meet you there, then." Noelle strode off down the street before Georgia or Daisy had a chance to object or try to change her mind.

She'd gone about a block when she heard a voice speak from behind her right shoulder. "Slow down, ma'am."

Did she know that voice?

"What are you doing here?" Noelle couldn't take her eyes off his handsome face and the way the evening air was blowing through his hair.

"Where else would I be?"

Noelle had never wanted anything in her life as much as she wanted Matt to reach out and take her in his arms. Oh, she knew it was crazy—she'd only met him less than a week ago, but she felt as though she'd known him her whole life.

Noelle looked at his smiling face, illuminated by the streetlight in front of the cathedral, and felt warm for the first time in a week. Finally, her feet weren't damp and her fingers weren't frozen. He reached up and pulled the scarf he'd given her closer to her throat.

"You've all just been at church?"

She nodded, somehow unable to find her voice. The Christmas lights in the trees across the street gleamed as the headlights from passing cars brought them in and out of the dark.

For the first time in almost a week there were no snow-flakes in the air, not on her hair, her cheeks, her eyelashes. The night sky seemed truly clear, even with all the streetlights and the office window lights that never went out. Clear, dry, crisp—it was a perfect night.

"The family wanted to take a taxi back to the hotel. I wanted to walk."

"I know. I saw them all get in the cab and I waited until it was gone."

They walked in silence for a block.

It was weird, but after all her eagerness to see him and to talk to him, she felt now as though she had all the time in the world. Time to tell him things, ask about things, about himself, his thoughts, his feelings, his ideas. And she knew that he'd answer every question.

They had to get it right, but they didn't have to do all that now.

He stared into her eyes, waiting for some kind of signal.

She tucked her arm into his, and it seemed just the right thing to do. As they walked along, Noelle gradually came out of her daze and noticed that he seemed weighed down on his right side by a huge department store bag.

"Were you just on your way home from shopping?" she asked.

"More or less," Matt said.

"Well, that doesn't answer my question." So strange, at her age, to be smiling and giggling with somebody.

"I think your real question is 'what's in the bag?'"

"It is."

"I'll show you soon enough. Maybe over there," he said, pointing toward a corner bar that was lit with a warm glow from the lights inside and the Christmas lights on its railing outside, "I'll tell you once we're out of the cold, with a good glass of Burgundy in front of us."

Noelle hugged his arm tighter. "I like your style."

He was in no hurry, though. They followed the server to two high-backed chairs in front of a blazing fire, he slid the bag under his chair, and then opened another unexpected, but completely compelling subject.

"Do you think we fell in love at first sight?" he said as comfortably as if he were discussing the Patriots' prospects in the playoff game coming up next week.

Noelle sputtered a little, her mouth half full of wine.

"Are you . . . . did we fall in love?"

"I did," Matt said, again so matter-of-factly that all her

shyness was disappearing. "When I saw you in the store that afternoon, wearing that coat and beaming at those little children, I just fell. I'm old enough now to recognize the feeling and not be afraid of it. "

"You're sure it wasn't my hysterical voice or my pale face when I realized that I'd managed to lose my four-year-old granddaughter? In a place packed with crowds? In New York City?"

Matt grinned. "Seriously, I found your concern for her quite attractive. I've always been a sucker for the nurturing, loving type. I'd rather have her around than the witty, sophisticated, smart-mouth, take-charge type any day." He savored his wine. "But that's not why I fell in love with you."

"Then why?"

"Guess," he said, pinning her with eyes so full of mischief and heat that she almost jumped over the table at him. 'I dare you', he seemed to be saying.

Well, game on.

"Because of the black knee-high boots with the heels?"

"I do love boots, but no."

"You like my hair? My eyes?"

"You are cute, and I like the way you look, yeah."

Noelle leaned forward with her elbows on the little table. The chemistry was irresistible. Simply.

"But that's not the reason," Matt said. "I fell in love with you because I felt like I'd known you forever. Like I was coming home." He raised his glass in a toast. "To innocence."

She raised an eyebrow at that. "If you'd asked me to guess what you were thinking, I'd never have picked 'innocence' in a hundred years."

"To innocence and to time. I'm feeling a bit sad that I didn't know you when we were both young."

"But we have all sorts of time now," Noelle said. The words were out of her mouth before she considered them, and as she heard them echo in the quiet of the bar, she knew. Yes, I did fall in love with him. I've been in love with him all along.

It was the reason she'd been so disturbed and so upset . . . were those the right words? So unlike herself, anyway.

"So, do you think we did?" he prompted her after the server had refreshed their glasses and then discreetly disappeared.

"Did what?" she asked, almost not hearing his question because she was so hypnotized by his dark blue eyes and the way his mouth curved on the right side.

"Fell in love at first sight."

"Is that a deal-breaker for you?" she teased. "Would it be too unromantic if it weren't at first sight? For both of us?"

"No, it would just be a different first-meeting story. Every couple has to have their story of how they met, don't you think? Memories of what their first words to each other were?" Matt took a sip of his wine. "And love at first sight is more likely when you're older, don't you think? Because we know more."

"My, you are romantic."

"Is that bad? Don't you like it?"

"I like everything about you."

He stared at her intently for a long moment. Maybe it was even five minutes, she didn't know. "I want to be somewhere alone with you," he said. "Right now."

"Matt, it's Christmas Eve. There's nowhere to go. I can't bring you back to my hotel. I don't want to share you with all those people."

He stared at her for a few more minutes, then finally said, "My place."

She could see that he was nervous about what her response might be. He didn't need to worry.

She nodded yes.

**

His apartment was only six blocks away. With every step, she felt brand new. She wanted to stop every person passing by, to tell them how wonderful she felt. Of course, even though it was Christmas Eve in Manhattan, that would have been quite a few conversations. Funny, but she'd watched so many movies, read so many books, and heard so many romantic songs, describing these feelings. She'd never realized it was the writer recounting something that had happened to him or her.

This feeling couldn't last, could it?

"Matt, are you sure you want the real me?" Noelle asked as she rushed along, trying to keep up with his long stride. "Someone like me . . . I come with a lot of baggage. The children, the grandchildren—"

"Noelle, you are you. I've been wanting you for a long time . . . for forever. Not someone like you. You. I just knew it. I know it. I've dated a lot of women and with most of them, I've had to do a sort of 'count up the score' thing. She has this, she doesn't have that, this is great, this is not so good. But with you, I just know."

Her phone buzzed and the call display showed Georgia's

name. Absolutely not. She tapped the "Ignore" button, then smiled at Matt. "I've decided not to let my daughters have any more of my Christmas Eve," she said. "It's ten o'clock and I've already spent most of the day with them. This time is mine."

Matt could see that she needed to stand her ground, but he had an eye on future diplomatic relations. "Maybe you could just text her. Once. Tell her you're fine, wish her a Merry Christmas, and that you won't be back tonight."

"I won't?"

"Not if you don't want to be. You're welcome to stay with me until morning." He kissed her, warmly and slowly. "So welcome."

A few minutes later, she came up for air. "Let me take a minute and send her that text," she said. "That was a good idea you had, Mr. Kezanski."

"One of many, I promise you, ma'am," he said as he released her. "Send the text."

Not more than ten seconds after she sent it, Georgia came back.

What about the kids' cookies to-night? It's the seventh tin. Can I give it to them? They're asking

I'll do it myself tomorrow morning when I'm back.

But they'll need cookies to leave for Santa

Ask Justin.

Who's that?

The chef. The kiddies will know.

Matt's condo floated high above Central Park; she could see the Plaza Hotel in the distance. His taste was contemporary, but not so many clean lines that it was a sketch instead of a painting. It was the perfect combination of style, charm, comfort, and luxury.

"I would like to make us a snack," he said. "Would you like a drink, too?"

"Maybe some wine?" Noelle leaned back against the leather couch and smiled at him. "You know, you're completely spoiling me. For so many years, I was the one putting food and drink together for the family. Lately, I've had only myself to cater to."

"But that's not nearly as nice as providing treats for someone else," Matt said. "Please, yes, let me spoil you."

He went off to the kitchen. Noelle could hear him opening the refrigerator door and taking things out of the cupboard.

She looked around the room, then enjoyed the view of New York's sparkling lights, so many floors below. He had enough seating for eight people, an enormous TV screen, and a wall of books that she intended to inspect as soon as she got the chance.

Her gaze fell on her phone, and she got an idea.

Matt's number was in her contacts. No photo yet— she made a mental note to take care of that soon.

Hey

From the kitchen, she heard his phone buzz and his movements stop. She pictured him pulling it from his pocket.

Matt laughed, and it was the most delightful sound she'd ever heard. Her stomach actually did a flip.

Hey yourself. Red or white?

Surprise me

The Bordeaux he poured was perfect and the charcuterie board that he brought out was as beautiful as any she'd seen in a restaurant. They nibbled and sipped in silence for a while, then Matt leaned back against the couch. "Let me show you what I have in the Christmas bag."

"Oh, yes, I forgot all about it! Show me now."

Matt lifted the department store bag to the couch between them. Noelle saw three identical parcels, brightly wrapped in Christmas paper.

She opened the first one and discovered a Mini GPT3. "Are they all the same?"

Matt nodded.

"Three of these robot toys? But how did you . . . ?"

"I am Señor Ricardo Juarez," Matt confessed. "I won this one in that snowman-building day in Bryant Park."

"But there are three of them here!"

"I also set it up with Harmonie Randolph to meet the decorator at the hotel and put in dibs on the one they were using for the Christmas Eve Buffet set up. They delivered it here just an hour ago."

"They said they had to keep it up there for Christmas dinner!"

He grinned. "I am persuasive."

Noelle stared at the shiny things inside their boxes.

Matt leaned back, both arms spread across the back of the couch, Clearly, he was enjoying this. "And I am the man who knows Santa's middle name."

"So, you won the one in the department store? Is that fair?

"What do you mean?"

"Well, if you're one of the honchos at the department store, or one of the owners or whatever, should you be winning things there?"

"I'm not one of the owners of the department store. Pamela Finch should get her facts straight before she speaks." Matt picked up the toy and inspected the packaging carefully. "Does it matter?"

Noelle took his face in her two hands. "It does not."

"I am also the man who is going to take up a lot of your time from now on."

"Are you moving to Vermont?"

"Are you moving to New York?"

Noelle sat up and took a long, measuring look. "We may have a problem here."

"We have no problem," Matt said. "Tell you what. Let's start with Christmas Eve and Christmas Day. Then maybe we'll celebrate New Year's. Then maybe take a little trip somewhere. Nobody has to move anywhere just yet."

Noelle relaxed. "That could work."

"We'll work it all out later. Together."

CHAPTER 17

Christmas morning dawned as clear as the night before, a perfect match for Noelle's mood. As she surfaced from a deep sleep, she was aware of his arms, still holding her from the night before. Had either of them stirred or moved an inch since they fell asleep?

She eased one eye open and then the other. His hair was rumpled and his face half-smiling; it looked like he was having a wonderful dream.

They hadn't closed the curtains the night before and through the window she could see no sign of the snow or drizzle that had fallen on the city during the week she'd been there. It was a lovely morning for . . . what? A long walk? More hours tangled up in sheets?

Her phone buzzed.

Or . . . a morning beside someone else's Christmas tree, watching while small children opened toys they might have forgotten by the first day of spring.

Noelle picked up the phone. Without opening his eyes,

Matt said, "Your sense of duty is staggering."

There was a smile in his voice, though, and she gave him a friendly push before she answered it.

"Hi, Georgia. Yes, I'm fine. You know I am. I sent you a text last night, and I told you I wouldn't be back until morning."

She listened for a moment, then said, "You know, Georgia, this is really quite funny. You're lecturing me now about staying out all night in a way I never lectured you after you were an adult. You never would have let me—"

Matt pulled away from her, gave her an affectionate pat on her tush, and jumped out of bed, then headed through the bedroom door. Toward the kitchen, she hoped. Coffee was definitely needed.

"And I'm not standing for it either, sweetie. I'll be back at the hotel in an hour or two. I have some things to do before then. Give the kiddies a hug for me. Merry Christmas!" She practically sang it, as she turned off her phone.

"What things?" Matt asked as he crawled back under the quilt.

"Do what you feel. Didn't somebody write that in a song?" she whispered between kisses.

She could tell from his breathing that she was having the same effect on him that he was on her. When they took a pause, he said, "You know, I've been dreaming about this for days. Maybe even years." A few more kisses. "Well, really, for my whole life."

She laughed. "I know what you mean."

And she did. Sure, she'd been happy during many moments with Ian. Was it wrong that his memory and his name should cross her mind while she was with another man?

But she hadn't known anything like this before. Nothing like this actual, physical feeling of excitement, mixed with a little aching and a lot of euphoria.

Maybe this was what the songs and poets meant when they spoke of feelings? Not the thoughts, the reactions, the expectations she was familiar with, but actual feelings?

When her mind clicked back into gear, another hour had gone by in what seemed like seconds. Noelle put on Matt's shirt and used his phone to find a music app to add some Christmas carols to the atmosphere.

"Do you want a hot breakfast? I have eggs, and I could do biscuits."

"In New York? Doesn't it have to be bagels?"

He grinned. "Yes, of course. I have bagels, too. Poppyseed, wholewheat, sourdough, and onion."

"Sounds perfect."

"All of them, ma'am?!"

"A taste of each. I've worked up an appetite, Mr. Kezanski," she said.

"You're not missing your traditional Christmas breakfast? I'll bet you had a long list of goodies that you served every year."

"I did, but I'm not missing it. You seem to have knocked everything out of my head completely."

He gazed at her. "Are you sure? It's Christmas morning . . . how are you feeling about not being there when the grandkids get out of bed and see what Santa brought?"

Noelle shook her head. "I've seen many a Christmas morning. I thought all I wanted was to be there each year, but it isn't. I want you. And this."

Matt smiled and gave her another hug. "What do you want to do after breakfast? Should we stick together? Go back to the hotel together?"

"You know, I think it would be better if I go see them first, get them used to the idea of seeing their mother acting like a teenager," she said.

"Come over here and let me get used to it, too," Matt said.

**

When Noelle walked into the hotel suite, the atmosphere was not festive. Kelsey and Kenneth were on the couch, watching TV, while Georgia and Kyle were on their phones.

"Nonny Noelle!" The kids jumped from the couch and ran to her.

"Hold it right there! Freeze!" she commanded.

They giggled, Kenneth in mid-stride, with both arms extended, and Kelsey with her right knee up by her cheek.

Noelle left them there, slipped into her walk-in closet/ bedroom for a moment and came out carrying the seventh, and final, tin of cookies. She pulled off the lid, then grinned at the two. "Unfreeze!"

And they were all over the cookies, each taking four or five in a handful and going off to munch while they watched TV.

"Georgia, Kyle. Merry Christmas. How did your morning go?" Noelle was determined to act as though nothing unusual was going on.

Georgia put down her phone. "Hi, Mom. It was just lovely. As you can see, the kids got a lot of new toys, and clothes, and books. How was yours?"

They looked at each other, Georgia with a mischievous glint in her eye, and they both giggled. Giggled. Really?

"I don't think you want the answer to that question," Noelle said.

Georgia smiled.

"I thought I might invite him to join us for the rest of the day. Is that all right with you?" Noelle asked.

"Yes, of course. But let's check with Daisy, too."

"Check with me about what?" Daisy wandered into the living room. "Merry Christmas, everybody." She frowned at her sister. Don't you have a ban on phones on Christmas Day, like I have at my house?"

"We need the phone. Come on, Daisy," Georgia said. "Even on Christmas Day, sometimes you have to communicate with other people. But it's not about work. I think Kyle is texting with his mother."

Noelle waited until Daisy and her family had their coats off, then gathered everybody in the living room of the suite. "I'm glad that you're all here. I want to give the little ones one more gift."

"Another gift? Mom, you've already given them their gifts," Georgia said.

"One more." Noelle reached into the bag and pulled out a mini-GPT3. "This is for you, Kenny."

Kenneth had his hands on the box before the words were out of her mouth. "A robot! A robot!"

Kelsey was right behind him, reaching for hers. Frost didn't know what was happening, but copying his older cousins always seemed like a good idea.

Noelle watched the thrill on their faces and felt that it had all been worth it. She didn't know whether this would be the year they received the Christmas gift they'd remember all their lives, but she did know she was happy to have been able to make their dreams come true this year, just in case this was it.

Thanks to Matt.

She also knew it was unlikely that one of the Christmas stories they'd remember all their lives would be their turkey dinner being lost to a pack of ravening dogs. Chef Justin had it under professional lock and key in the kitchen, and she was looking forward to the feast this afternoon. She had more appetite than she'd had in months—years, maybe!

But it was hours until dinner. "What's the plan?" Noelle asked.

"We don't want to just hang around the hotel all day, so the plan is—"

"Skay-ting! Skay-ting!" Kenneth had been listening to their conversation and was leading the chorus.

Noelle laughed. "Okay, skating."

CHAPTER 18

The rink at Rockefeller Center was packed with skaters, a scene that sur-prised Noelle. On Christmas Day? Apparently so—and of course, here they were, too, so why should she be surprised that many other people had found their way there?

The snow began to fall soon after they arrived, and Noelle was glad she'd thought to bring along her scarf. The one that Matt had given her. The one tangible piece of evidence she had of the whole thing happening. At some moments, she felt as though she'd imagined everything.

Then she saw him walking toward her through the crowd around the hot chocolate stand. There was her other tangible piece of evidence.

"I'm happy to see you, stranger."

"I'm happy to see you, too."

But the voice was not Matt's. Right behind him, over his shoulder, the black orb of a TV lens intruded into her space, just as Dan Keyes, microphone in hand, put a hand on her shoulder and turned her toward the camera.

"This is my final feature of the week, Noelle. I'd be honored if you would agree to let me put you and your grand-children in the public eye, show the world what a lovely family you have, what a devoted grandma you are."

Noelle looked at him. She was not going to allow him to bowl her over. "I know what a lovely family I have, Dan, and I don't really care if anybody else in the world knows it."

"Daniel, stop pestering the lady." Matt had stepped forward to grip her elbow.

"She's not your lady, Matthew."

Noelle looked back and forth between the two men. There was an odd tone going on here. "Do you two know each other?"

The standoff went on for about ten seconds before the cameraman broke into it. "I'm outa here, boss," he said to Dan. "This has nothing to do with a Channel 45 story."

The three of them watched the back of the chubby man's winter jacket disappear into the crowd of onlookers around the skating rink.

"Alright, tell me what's going on, Matt," Noelle said. It was a good thing that Georgia, Daisy, and their families were on the other side of the rink, getting their skates. There were enough curious bystanders without being related to any of them.

"You should have told her before now, Matt," Dan said.

"Told me what?"

Matt glanced back and forth between them, one ac-cusing and one cautious, if not downright suspicious. Then, he seemed to decide not to buy in to the drama. Where was it coming from, anyway? Only Dan.

"Nothing much to tell," he said. "This is my brother, Daniel."

On some subconscious level, Noelle noticed the people standing within earshot nudge each other and settle in to watch. She stared at Matt's face.

"Your brother."

"Yes, my brother. He decided he was ashamed of the family name at some point, and he changed it to Keyes."

"My editor asked. Forty years ago. In Denver," Dan said.

"We both live in New York now. We have different lives."

"That's an understatement," Dan said. "He's retired. I'll be working till I drop."

"Come on, Daniel, she barely knows you. She shouldn't have to get acquainted with your bitterness and your game-playing just because she's getting to know me," Matt said. "And she shouldn't have had to put up with your pressure all week because of that, either."

"I always like to stay on top of your activities, little brother. You know that. And I'd say it's a little more than getting to know you. You said she's the one."

Noelle thought she imagined a collective gasp go through the crowd, which was now about three rows thick surrounding them. On the fringes near the hot dog truck, she thought she saw Daisy and Georgia. She felt Matt's hands grip her arms.

"Noelle! It's alright. I'm here now. Where's your family?

How did the robot toys go over with the kids?"

She heard his words, but she was in a fog. He knew how pressured she'd felt about Dan's urging her to be in his TV feature, and he could have done something to make that go away. He could have at least told her about their connection. Obviously, he'd been talking to Dan about her—why couldn't he have talked to her about Dan?

Where was his loyalty?

"Noelle?"

She couldn't answer.

"Noelle, it's too bad you had to find out this way," Dan said. "I was all for telling you on day one, when I bumped into you both in the department store. But he wanted some time . . . time to make his move, I said. But he said, no, time to get to know her."

"I did get to know you," Matt said, looking into her eyes. "And I think there's a lot more to get to know."

"Mom?" Georgia's voice floated over the crowd of strangers and Noelle turned toward her.

"Let's let her sort it out." Daisy's voice was softer, but it was amazing to Noelle that her younger one was telling the big sister to shut up.

Noelle was still stumped for words. She looked back and forth between the two, remembering how harassed she'd felt by Dan's repeated requests for her permission to film her. How she'd stewed about whether this would be good for the grandkids, and for the family. How she'd wondered if she was over-reacting to everything. Now, she was finding out that Dan Keyes had been gaslighting her. Matt knew it and did nothing to stop it.

"No!" She shook Matt's hands off her arms. "This is something you should have, and could have, told me days ago. That he's your brother, that there was this other reason he was pushing me to let him into my life. I wondered why he was being so persistent. God! There must be a million other grandmothers in New York this week."

She took two steps backward from Matt. "Why didn't you tell me?"

He looked miserable. "Because I thought you'd react this way. And I wanted just a little more time for us to find out what this was about before we had to let things get heavy. I've been waiting for so long and I just didn't want to take a chance on losing it. I guess I just didn't know what was the right thing to do.

Was it a good enough reason?

His eyes were so intense that she felt they were drilling into her. "I've been to a lot of places, Noelle, and met a lot of people, during all my years at the hospital. I thought I'd seen everything, but I hadn't seen you."

He waited for her to speak, then rushed in to fill the silence when she didn't. "Please. You are . . . you are . . . necessary, Noelle. That's what you are. You're necessary. We have to give this a try. Please. Could we?"

He waited, but she couldn't speak.

"Alright," Matt said. "I get it. I made a mistake."

Dan had slipped away into the crowd of onlookers. Matt turned to go. If I let him walk away, the pain will be worse. Noelle reached out for his coat sleeve.

He stopped and turned back. She stared into his eyes, then spoke. "Uh-oh."

He blinked. "Yeah. Absolutely. Uh-oh. Oops."

"Not something you want to hear your surgeon say." The edges of Noelle's mouth were twitching. Upward. "Not your guy in charge of two hundred other surgeons, either."

"But perfectly okay coming from somebody realizing they've fallen hard." Matt stared at her for a few moments, then read the invitation in her eyes. He took the two steps toward her and swept her into his arms.

The ring of skaters around them put their hands together and gave them a round of applause.

CHAPTER 19

Matt slammed the trunk shut and brushed the snow off the license plate on the vintage Mercedes 500 SL. He had two suitcases, two overnight bags, and an extra blanket tucked in tight.

"Are you ready to try out California?" he asked Noelle, after settling himself into the driver's seat. He reached over to buckle her in.

"Are you?" she asked. "Tell me again why we're driving there?"

"Because it's a tie-breaker, between Burlington and New York. Neither one of us has ever been there, and we both want to see it. And we both like a road trip."

She beamed as he started the car. "I'm ready to go anywhere with you."

Matt turned to look into her eyes. "I don't know if you really get it, sweetheart. I was just walking around, waiting for life to start up again, before that afternoon at that department store. You saved me, do you understand?"

"Tell me again."

"I will, again and again. You won't ever have to ask, or even wonder, if I still feel the same. I'll tell you so often you might get sick of it."

"You might get sick of saying it."

"The only ones who get tired of saying it are the ones who don't feel it."

She leaned in for a kiss, and as usual, he didn't disappoint. "If we stay here much longer, they'll tow us away," she said.

As he put it in gear and pulled away from the curb, Noelle was pulling a tin from her bag.

"What's this?"

"California is a long drive. We'll need food."

"Cookies aren't food."

"Yes, they are."

Matt pulled the car back over the curb. "I was going to wait until at least lunch time for this. But since you've dropped the flag on it so early, I'll do my part."

He opened the door and got out of the car.

Noelle twisted around in her seat to see what he was doing. He went to the trunk, opened it, and then closed it again. When he got back into his seat, he was carrying a small cooler.

"What is it?"

"Take a look."

Whatever she was expecting, she wouldn't have guessed this. She saw seven small containers, each with a sticky note labeled with a day of the week. She opened them, one by one: Gruyere, Brie, Cheddar, Gouda, Pecorino, Stilton, and Swiss.

"How do you know I will want to eat one for each of the seven days?" she teased him. "How do you know I won't want to eat them all in one afternoon?"

"How about making them last longer?" he asked as he put the car into gear and pulled out into traffic. "How about seven years instead of seven days? And if you can't make them last that long, I know where we can get more."

ABOUT DEVIN AUDRAH

Devin Audrah is an ardent writer and a believer in romance. Born in south Florida, she has lived in eleven cities and visited fifty states, ten provinces, and seventeen countries. She loves chocolate, classic rock, roses, and fine wine.

She visits New York City as frequently as she can.

If you enjoyed *SEASON'S MEETINGS*, we'd love to see an online review and rating.

Please join our email newsletter list to find out about Devin's upcoming books. You can sign up at
www.windwordgroup.com.

You can read more about her work at
www.devinaudrah.com.